A Toast to Murder

A Myrtle Clover Cozy Mystery, Volume 24

Elizabeth Spann Craig

Published by Elizabeth Spann Craig, 2024.

A TOAST TO MURDER

First edition. April 9, 2024.

Written by Elizabeth Spann Craig.

Chapter One

"Miles, you're hydrated enough."

Miles gave his friend Myrtle a steady look. "Dehydration can be very serious. And we're about to attend a wine tasting."

"You must have drunk a gallon of water. You'll be in the restroom the whole tasting, at this rate. Besides, the winery will have tiny little glasses for us to drink from. It won't be enough to dehydrate a flea."

"Regardless, I want to be prepared. I'm also bringing a stainless-steel water bottle. I recommend you do the same."

"Phooey on that. I've had a full glass of water and that will be plenty, I'm sure."

Miles said, "I'd like to go over the driving arrangements."

"Again? I thought we went over this."

"Yes, but I like to be absolutely sure of a plan when there's drinking involved," said Miles, pushing his glasses up his nose.

Myrtle sighed. "As I said the other day, I'm not much of a tippler, so I'll be the one driving back home. Elaine is driving us there. That way, you and Elaine can drink as much as you like, and I'll have a small sip of wine and drive us safely home."

Miles carefully avoided mentioning the fact that the ride home was sure to be a slow one, at least. Myrtle's speed of choice was thirty miles an hour, and that's if she was in a hurry. Instead, he said, "I'm still not very sure about drinking at eleven a.m. I don't think I've ever had a drink before noon in my life."

"Not even a bloody Mary? Or a mimosa?"

"Have you?" asked Miles.

"No. But then, we've already established that I'm not much of a tippler. However, I think you should live a little. Remember, we're doing this for Elaine. She's absolutely thrilled about going to this winery." Elaine was Myrtle's daughter-in-law. She and Red, Myrtle's son, lived across the street from her with her grandson, Jack.

Miles said, "Right. The new wine tasting hobby. At least that shouldn't result in any unwanted arts or crafts being foisted on us."

"Precisely. And it's a hobby she can engage in by herself, which is lovely. All she has to do is keep a variety of different wines in the house. It's finally a hobby that Red can stand behind, too."

"And Jack is coming with us to the tasting?" asked Miles. "Should we be packing up the trucks and blocks from the toy box in your closet?"

"No, Jack has a playdate with a preschool friend of his. The mom is paying Elaine back for watching her son a week ago. Besides, we won't be gone all day. Preschool playdates are only for a couple of hours at the most. Otherwise, chaos reigns." Myrtle glanced around her house, making a face. "Sort of like my home right now."

Miles's gaze lit on the dusty tables, the dust bunnies huddled against the baseboards, and the kitchen floor, which was crying out to be mopped. "Puddin problems again?" Puddin was Myrtle's lackadaisical housekeeper.

"Puddin *is* a problem," muttered Myrtle. "I haven't been able to lure her here for weeks.

"What about Dusty?" Dusty was Myrtle's yardman and married to Puddin. The two of them were a package deal. Unfortunately, the package was often tricky to get delivered.

"Both members of the undynamic duo appear to be screening their calls." Myrtle gritted her teeth, then regarded Miles. He was taking another large gulp from his water. "Why don't *you* call Puddin?"

"I can't think what that will accomplish."

Myrtle said, "Puddin will answer if you call. Then I can grab your phone and get her over here. The mess is driving me insane."

Miles sighed, pulled out his phone, and located Puddin's contact information. He called her from time to time when his own housekeeper couldn't make it. To Myrtle's frustration, Puddin always did an amazing job cleaning Miles's house. It was all quite unfair.

Puddin answered right away. "Mr. Miles?"

Myrtle jerked the phone out of his hand. "It's Myrtle Clover, Puddin."

Puddin snarled, "You tricked me."

"Deservedly. I haven't seen hide nor hair of you or Dusty for weeks. My house and yard are in shambles."

"You should learn to pick up after yourself," said Puddin in a self-righteous voice.

Myrtle gritted her teeth. "You know very well that clutter isn't the problem. It's dust and grime. Which is exactly what I need your help with. Now come on over here and do your job. Dusty too."

"You're not the boss of us!"

Myrtle said, "It's completely obvious that no one is the boss of you, including you. The two of you have no self-discipline whatsoever. I've got an event to attend this morning, but when I come back, I want the house cleaned and the grass mowed. I'm going to leave a helpful list to ensure that all the things are taken care of. You have a key."

"Don't know where it is," growled Puddin.

"You'd better find it and come over here. I don't want a key to my house just floating around out there."

Puddin said sullenly, "Usually you keep them things under one of yer gnomes."

"Well, last time I stupidly handed it to you instead. And none of my gnomes are in the yard, currently."

Puddin snorted. "Red's behaving hisself?"

"Somewhat."

Miles smiled. He was sure that, knowing Red, an infraction was forthcoming.

"Now locate the key and come over," said Myrtle in a peremptory tone. She hung up the phone.

Miles only had the time to drink a couple more sips of water and refill his water bottle when Elaine tapped on Myrtle's door. Her eyes were shining. "Ready for a fun adventure?"

Myrtle wasn't at all sure there was anything at all adventurous about drinking. The few times in her life that she'd overindulged, she found herself in an unhappy adventure in the ladies' room. But she saw how excited Elaine was about the wine tasting and said in her most convincing voice, "So ready! Aren't you ready, Miles?"

Miles nodded his head. He said, "I understand you're driving there and Myrtle is driving back."

"How tiresome of you, Miles!" said Myrtle. "I just confirmed the plan with you a minute ago."

Elaine beamed at Miles. "It's always a good idea to make sure. Yes, you and I won't be driving home, so we can really indulge at the tasting. I'm planning to try the entire flight of wines, then have a glass of my favorite. But I'll likely be spitting out a lot of the wine."

"You think it'll be bad?" Miles looked concerned.

Elaine smiled at him. "No, I mean that I'll try to mimic real wine tasters. They smell the wine, look at how the wine spins in the glass, then they swish the wine in their mouths and spit it out. They don't consume much alcohol that way."

They walked out to Elaine's minivan as Elaine chatted happily about the wine tasting. Myrtle was glad to see that Elaine had apparently vacuumed out the vehicle and there were no Cheerios in sight. Miles sat in the back, carefully strapping himself in with the seatbelt.

"North Carolina wines have really been winning some awards lately," said Elaine in a cheerful voice. She talked about muscadine wines and wineries that sourced their grapes elsewhere, but concocted delicious beverages from them.

Myrtle thought rather uncharitably that Elaine was once again inflicting her hobby on them. But then again, as Miles had deftly pointed out, this particular hobby wasn't as onerous as many of the others. And she so rarely spent time with her daughter-in-law without Jack there. Myrtle adored Jack and was certain he was gifted. But Elaine was always very distracted when Jack was near her. Her conversations around Jack were disjointed, abbreviated, confusing, or a stream of consciousness, depending on the day. Her monologue about the North Carolina wine industry was perhaps the most coherent thing she'd heard Elaine say in a while.

Myrtle said, "And remind me again about this winery. You had a connection there, is that right?"

"Exactly. The owner, Isabella Montague, is a friend of mine and invited me to come out. The winery has just recently opened, and this is an event to generate interest and buzz. It's going to be a beautiful morning."

Miles cleared his throat from the back of the minivan. "We'll be indoors, I'm guessing?" There was a hopeful tone to his voice. It was mid-October, a lovely time to be outside . . . for brief intervals. There was also a robust wind, which was tossing around some leaves that had fallen from the trees. Having spent a lot of time around Miles, Myrtle knew he was worried that he hadn't put on enough warm clothing. With the slightest encouragement from the meteorologists, Miles would sling a scarf around his neck, a woolen hat on his head, and gloves on his hands.

"Oh, I think so, don't you? Unless there's absolutely no room at all inside. Isabella said something about firepits. That might be fun," said Elaine.

Myrtle very much doubted a firepit would be fun. She had the terrible feeling it might entail sitting on a backless bench of some sort. Her back was generally cooperative unless Myrtle asked too much of it.

Before long, they reached the winery. The outside was quite impressive. It looked as if someone had money and that money had lovingly gone into creating the business. The exterior was made of weathered wood and stone, blending seamlessly with the vineyard surrounding it. The main entrance boasted a large wooden door with wrought-iron details. There was a wrap-around porch supported by wooden columns and some inviting-looking rocking chairs.

"Wow, this is pretty upscale," said Elaine as she parked the minivan. "I had no idea it was such a big operation. I thought it was just a small tasting room with an acre of muscadines. This looks like a ski lodge in Aspen or something."

The inside was just as impressive. There was a massive stone fireplace surrounded by cozy armchairs. The walls were adorned with photos showing the winemaking process. The ceilings had exposed wooden beams, and there were enormous picture windows providing views of the vineyard.

"Very nice," said Myrtle. She was eyeing the armchairs in front of the fireplace. They were currently occupied, but she hoped she could take over as soon as the guests placed another drink order or got up to use the restroom.

There were more people attending the tasting than Myrtle had expected. Miles was apparently thinking the same thing. There must have been thirty or more people there. "I had no idea the Bradley area contained so many early drinkers," he murmured.

"Well, we're joining them today," said Myrtle with a glare. "For Elaine's sake."

Elaine was looking around, trying to find her friend. She returned to them saying, "Isabella has got to be swamped right now. I'll catch up with her when she has time. In the meantime, let's get started. I'll order our flights."

Myrtle wasn't completely sure of the terminology, although she'd now heard the word "flight" twice and was sure Elaine wasn't planning on airplane rides anytime soon. Her confusion cleared when Elaine returned from the bar carrying two boards with small glasses of wine nestled into holes cut into the wood.

"Sure we don't need a third?" asked Elaine.

"No, no," said Myrtle. "I'll have a small sip from one or two of the wines on Miles's."

Miles looked rather unhappy to hear this news.

"For heaven's sake, Miles. I'm completely germ free."

"Lots of people think they're germ free," said Miles gloomily. "But they're actually infectious and don't start having symptoms until later."

Elaine said, "Myrtle, you can share mine."

"No, dear, it's your tasting. Tell you what—how about if I just stay completely sober and enjoy the ambiance? I'll experience the tasting through your perceptions of the wines, Elaine."

Myrtle turned and looked grimly at the people hogging the armchairs. "But I'm going to insist on those chairs."

Fortunately, one of the people rose to get a glass of wine while another in the party left for the restroom. The third was too intent on his phone to object when they sat in the three armchairs. By the time the others returned, the last remaining member of their party sheepishly left them to it.

There was a sizeable coffee table in front of the grouping of chairs. It was perfect for resting the flights on. Elaine was enthusiastically trying the wines, spitting them out in some sort of spittoon thing, then jotting down notes in a small notebook she'd brought with her. Miles was more cautiously sipping each, taking several minutes to finish a single sample.

"Which one is the winner for you, Elaine?" asked Miles politely. He was still carefully swilling the second glass of the flight.

"Gosh, that's a tough one. I'd say it's between the rosé blend or the sparkling." Then Elaine embarked on a list of technical wine-judging-type phrases that quickly lost Miles and Myrtle's attention.

Elaine finally wrapped it up with, "But I think I want my full glass to be that vanilla mead. That was amazing."

Myrtle said, "Better go grab it while the bartender is free, my dear. I'll guard your seat." And indeed, Myrtle's face so quickly assumed a ferocious expression that no one even thought about venturing near.

Elaine came back beaming, the glass of mead in her hands. "I saw Isabella up there. She's the one with the pretty chestnut-colored hair."

Myrtle and Miles dutifully looked over to find Isabella. The young woman, dressed in a burgundy knee-length dress with leather boots, gave them a wave from across the room. Then she was whisked away by a customer.

Elaine said, "She's *so* excited by the turnout. I don't blame her. There are tons more people here than I thought there would be."

Elaine happily chatted about Isabella and other friends, the adorable things preschooler Jack was doing these days, and her plans on getting Red to Serenity Springs by hook or by crook. She only needed to convert Red from beer to wine.

After Elaine finished her wine, she said, "I'm going to stop by the gift shop for a minute, if that's okay with the two of you?"

Miles, who still had two tiny wine tastings to do, nodded drowsily. It looked as if he might drift off to sleep in front of the fireplace before he could finish his flight. Myrtle said, "Have fun, Elaine. I'll just rest my bones for a few minutes."

Miles did indeed catnap, his chin falling to his chest. Myrtle contented herself with looking around the large tasting room while Elaine shopped. It wasn't long before Elaine returned with a smile and a shopping bag. Miles woke with a start, looking guilty at his sudden nap.

"I saw this in the gift shop and couldn't resist," said Elaine. "It's a thank you, Myrtle, for helping with Jack all the time."

"A present?" Myrtle perked up. She quickly opened the bag and pulled out a particularly fetching gnome. She crooned, "Look at him! What a little darling."

The darling gnome was cheerful and rotund. His small hat had tiny grapes and a grapevine pattern on it. He sported a tunic with wine glasses and grape clusters painted on, and a mischievous smile. Naturally, he was holding a wine glass.

"Won't Red be annoyed you gave him to me?" asked Myrtle, cradling the gnome.

"That's what makes this such perfect timing! He won't have to know."

Myrtle gave a pleased smile. "Indeed, he won't. And the timing is even better than you thought. I was going to give one of my old gnomes as a donation to Greener Pastures Retirement Home. I felt the grounds there could use a touch of whimsy. This little guy will fill the gap in my collection perfectly. Thank you, Elaine." She carefully put the gnome back in the shopping bag.

Elaine glanced across the room and sighed. "I really don't want to leave without introducing you both to Isabella."

It seemed to be an impossible task. The Serenity Springs owner was clearly inundated with customers and friends, all vying for her attention. She wanted to please Elaine, but she had also secretly been hoping to get back home shortly to watch the tape of her soap opera, *Tomorrow's Promise*. Plus, Miles appeared to be falling asleep again. Myrtle could understand—it was becoming rather stuffy in the tasting room between the fire, her coat, and the number of people inside.

"How about if we kill time for a few minutes outside? I wouldn't mind a breath of cool air, and it would be nice to see the vineyard closer up."

Elaine brightened at the suggestion. "Great idea. I'd like to see the vineyard, too. What about Miles, though?"

Miles was now puffing out tiny snores from his pursed lips.

"I think we should leave Miles in here. He's not fond of brisk wind, and I see branches moving out there."

Elaine looked uncertain. "Won't he be alarmed if he wakes up and we're not anywhere around?"

"I'm sure he'll know we haven't forgotten him," said Myrtle. Then she considered this further since Elaine continued making the doubtful face. "I'll leave a note for him." She pulled a small notepad out of her large purse, fishing out a pen from the depths of the bag. Then she scribbled *Gone outside to get air* on a piece of paper that she placed in Miles's lap. "There," she said in satisfaction. "Now he'll be just fine."

So she and Elaine headed out the back door of the tasting room onto the veranda. There were indeed firepits. Fortunately, they were flanked by chairs with actual backs on them, instead of the backless benches Myrtle had feared. There were also several people outside, chatting and drinking wine. One man looked the mirror image of Miles and was dozing, body slumped in front of the firepit.

Myrtle and Elaine took a short stroll, Myrtle leaning heavily on her cane on the uneven ground among the vines. The vines' leaves were yellow, an apparent preface to losing them for the winter.

After a few minutes of walking and with no sign yet of Miles, Myrtle said, "Want to sit by the firepit for a few minutes? Perhaps people will begin leaving to get lunch and we'll have a chance to meet your friend."

They settled themselves in front of the fire. Myrtle kept looking curiously over at the sleeping man across from her. He had a spiky Van Dyke beard and equally spiky gray hair, perhaps from some sort of gel. But she couldn't see his face. And she was thinking he was slumped at a most peculiar angle for someone who was sleeping. Surely someone would wake up if they were in such an uncomfortable position.

Elaine followed Myrtle's gaze. She gave Myrtle a wry look. "Probably had too much to drink."

Myrtle frowned. "I think I know that man."

"Do you?"

"Gerald Greystone," said Myrtle, frowning deeper now. "Winemaker and wine critic."

Elaine looked more carefully at the man. "Well, those seem like suitable occupations for him. He appears to enjoy wine quite a bit."

Myrtle leaned over to call to the man. "Gerald. Gerald Greystone!"

There was no response. A man from a nearby group gave Myrtle an amused look.

Myrtle got up from her chair and walked across to the man. She put her hand out and shook his shoulder.

When Gerald slumped even further, it was clear that he was dead.

Chapter Two

Not only was Gerald Greystone quite deceased, and due to his body's contortions, it appeared that he might have had a very unpleasant demise. His expression said *strychnine* to Myrtle. She backed up and looked grimly at Elaine. "You'll need to call Red. And we'll need to get everyone away from the area."

Elaine gaped at her for a second before dialing her husband, who was the chief of police. As she did, Myrtle spoke loudly in her best teacher's voice. "There's been a suspicious death. The police are on their way. Everyone must stay on the grounds, but you'll need to step inside, away from the body."

At the mention of a body, everyone sent shocked glances toward the slumped man, then hurried off for the tasting room.

Elaine finished her call as she and Myrtle followed the others to the tasting room. There was lots of background chatter going on inside. People stood huddled by the fire, talking to each other and gesturing to the outside. The staff looked confused, asking each other what had happened.

Miles looked the most confused of all. He'd just woken up from a lovely nap to find a note in his lap, no sign of his friends, and the building buzzing about a sudden death.

"What happened?" he asked blearily as he hurried over to Myrtle and Elaine.

"Gerald Greystone is dead," said Myrtle in a clipped voice. "Poisoned."

Miles, who had never finished his wine flight, still froze.

"Elaine, do you see your friend Isabella? She'll want to know what's going on."

Elaine craned her head to look around. "She's right over there," she said, gesturing toward the front door of the lodge.

Isabella Montague was frowning, listening to several guests who were gesticulating wildly as they talked. Myrtle strode over to her, cane thumping as she walked, with Elaine and Miles in tow.

"May I speak to you for a second?" she asked. "I'm Myrtle Clover, Elaine's mother-in-law." The surrounding guests quickly dispersed, still talking among themselves.

Isabella gave her a tense smile. "Oh, Miss Myrtle. Elaine told me so much about you." Isabella was looking quite stressed, as was understandable. However, saying just the right thing seemed like muscle memory to her. She was nervously fingering her necklace, which had a grapevine motif.

Myrtle pulled her away from the group of people and said quietly, "Gerald Greystone. You know him?"

"Of course," she said, frowning. "Is he all right? I've been hearing all kinds of things from people. What's happened?"

"He's dead. Out in front of your firepit," said Myrtle.

Isabella looked at Elaine and Miles for confirmation, not wanting to believe it. Elaine nodded, and Miles, who'd only just learned about the death, looked carefully noncommittal.

Myrtle said, "What's more, it appears he's been murdered."

"Murdered?" hissed Isabella frantically. "That's impossible."

"Red's on his way," said Elaine, giving her a sympathetic smile. "He told me on the phone to make sure everyone stays put until they can find out what happened and get statements."

Isabella swayed on her feet, looking pale. "I can't believe this."

"Let's go sit down," said Elaine, giving her friend a concerned look.

But Isabella shook her head. "I'd rather the guests sit. This isn't what anyone signed up for when they came for the tasting." She paused. "Excuse me, I should go out back and see what's happened. I'll be right back."

Myrtle put her hand out. "The police won't want anything disturbed."

Isabella gave her a quick nod. "I'll be careful." She strode to the back door of the winery, ignoring customers who tried to speak with her. She was only out there for less than a minute before re-entering and joining Myrtle, Miles, and Elaine again. Isabella's face was troubled. She glanced around the room for a moment as if looking at all of her guests through a different lens.

"This is unbelievable," she said slowly. "How could something like this happen? And why would someone murder him here? We haven't been open long enough for most people to know we're even here."

"How long has the winery been open?" asked Miles.

Isabella gave an unhappy laugh. "Only six weeks. Oh my gosh, this is going to be the kiss of death for the place. The negative publicity alone is going to kill it. And I've put so much time and money into setting it all up." She paused. "I'm sorry, I know it's crass to consider money when someone has lost his life."

Miles wasn't listening to Isabella. The idea of poison was apparently still deeply embedded in his mind. He eyed his abandoned flight suspiciously, as if afraid it was going to explode.

Isabella turned to Myrtle. "You say it looked like he'd been murdered. You're not sure?"

"Well, I'm not a coroner, but it certainly doesn't appear anything like a natural death to me. Did you know Gerald well? His vineyard adjoins yours, doesn't it?"

"It does. But I wouldn't say I knew him well." She gave Myrtle a look of concern, taking in Myrtle's advanced years and the cane. She made the leap that Myrtle must be horribly traumatized. Isabella reached out to her, gently taking her arm. "I'm so sorry. You found him? That must have been an awful shock. Would *you* like to sit down? Maybe have a glass of wine?"

Miles, still clearly ruminating on the poison, gave Isabella an alarmed look.

Myrtle said, "No, I'm all right, thank you. At least, I'm doing much better than poor Gerald." Finding bodies, even traumatic looking ones, had become all too familiar for Myrtle. She glanced over at the door through narrowed eyes. "People are trying to leave, Isabella. Perhaps you should make sure they stay on the premises until the police give the okay?"

Isabella ran a hand through her hair and hurried over to the door. She spoke to the customers, who seemed quite annoyed at having to stay. Then she raised her voice. "Let me remind you we've all been asked by the police to stay here until they allow us to leave. I apologize for the inconvenience."

"It's a bit more than an inconvenience," murmured Miles.

"How well did you know Gerald?" Elaine asked Myrtle. "I know you recognized him right away."

"Oh, he and I were just acquaintances, really. I wrote a profile on him for the paper once after he gave Sloan some advertising dollars. The winery he owns is directly next to this one. I don't believe he was involved in the day-to-day running of it any longer, though. He'd employed a manager."

Elaine said in a quiet voice, "What do you think happened to him? Out there?" She gestured to the outdoors. The weather outside remained beautiful—sunlight pouring down out of blue skies. It created a strange backdrop for murder.

"I believe, just from looking at Gerald's contorted features, that he might have been poisoned with strychnine."

Miles and Elaine stared at her.

"Are you sure?" asked Miles. "You sound like you're a character in an Agatha Christie novel."

"I practically *am* a character in an Agatha Christie novel. Miss Marple. Although she was a mere child compared to me," said Myrtle with a sniff.

Miles clutched his water bottle to his chest as if concerned someone would come over and forcibly pour a noxious substance in there. "I'd imagine strychnine would be challenging to acquire these days."

"Not having been in the market for it, I wouldn't know," said Myrtle. "But yes, I'd think it's probably considered a controlled substance."

Isabella, after speaking with several guests along the way and trying to keep everyone calm, joined them again. She looked very pale and shaken. "I hope Red will make it here soon. People are getting restless." She glanced toward the back door. "Who's going to visit the winery if someone's been murdered here?" She sighed. "Aside from some really ghoulish folks."

"I'm sure the police will find out what's happened as quickly as possible," said Myrtle.

Isabella suddenly looked very focused on Myrtle. "Wait. You write for the newspaper, don't you?"

Myrtle was always pleased to be recognized as a reporter. "I do."

"You're going to write an article about this, aren't you?" Isabella nervously twisted her hands together. "About what happened?"

Naturally, she was. Myrtle lived to do crime reporting instead of wasting her time on the helpful hints column her editor made her do. She'd much rather be penning a serious story than turning in yet another article extolling the virtues of baking soda and white vinegar. "I'm sure Sloan will ask me to cover Gerald's death. This will be a big story, unfortunately."

Isabella said in a pleading voice, "Could you say something good about the winery in the article you write? Something about the wines, maybe? Or the building and the atmosphere?"

Miles cast a disbelieving look her way. Myrtle agreed with him. The atmosphere had certainly been shattered by the advent of murder.

"The story will be about Gerald, of course. But I can do a separate piece on your vineyard and winery. And a bit about you, of course. More of a profile piece."

Isabella seemed pleased. "Would you? That would be amazing."

"Of course. I'll come back soon and sit down to speak with you about it." Myrtle went into crime reporter mode. "Now, did you notice anything unusual today? Did anyone seem as if they didn't quite belong? Did you see anything that now might seem suspicious?"

Isabella was already shaking her head as Myrtle was speaking. "I've spent the whole time flitting around from one guest to another. Taking drink orders, promoting the wines. Talking about the vineyard. I didn't even go outside to the firepit—I was too busy inside."

Myrtle couldn't help but think that this was awfully convenient. After all, there were guests out there, too. And empty glasses to be collected. Plus, she'd seen a flicker in Isabella's eyes that made her think she wasn't completely telling the truth. "You didn't make it out there at all during the tasting? It seemed very tidy out there. I didn't see many empty glasses."

Isabella flushed. "You're right, actually. I did make it outside once and spotted Gerald there. He was talking with a couple of other customers. I just grabbed the empty glasses and headed back inside."

"Gerald has been focusing on his work as a wine critic lately, hasn't he?" asked Myrtle. "Did you invite him here today to write about the Serenity Springs wines?"

Isabella nodded. "I wanted Gerald to have a pleasant visit today. A good review from him could have meant a lot of extra business coming my way."

Miles cleared his throat. “How did Gerald handle being a wine critic and running a vineyard at the same time?”

“He wasn’t really hands-on at the vineyard anymore. He’d hired a guy, Ben Foster, to help him out. From everything I’ve heard, Ben’s doing an exceptional job at Greystone Grapes.” Isabella’s voice was just the tiniest bit bitter. Myrtle wondered if perhaps Isabella had tried hiring Ben to help at Serenity Springs instead.

Isabella continued, “I really like Ben. He’s a smart guy, very professional, with a lot going for him. He’s spent a little time over here, actually, and has been nice enough to give me some free advice.”

Myrtle raised her eyebrows. “What did Gerald think of that? His employee helping his competitor?”

Isabella flushed. “When he caught wind of it, he shut that down. Ben had been complaining about Gerald lately, as a matter of fact. I was wondering if he was going to end up quitting. Of course, I’d have been delighted to take Ben on over here.”

Elaine asked, “Why was Ben complaining about Gerald? The two of them didn’t get along?”

“Not lately, they haven’t. Apparently, the two of them had very different ideas for the future of Gerald’s vineyard. Ben didn’t care much for Gerald’s ideas.” Isabella paused, a small smile tugging at her lips. “Maybe now Ben will come over to work for me.”

Myrtle said carefully, “You don’t think Ben could have anything to do with Gerald’s death, do you?”

"What? No. No, of course not. I can't picture him being violent. He's just very passionate about grape growing and sustainability in the grape growing industry. He couldn't harm a fly."

But Myrtle saw that flicker in Isabella's eyes again. She'd like to hear more about her thoughts on Ben and Gerald's relationship. Before she could inquire further, however, Red suddenly showed up in uniform, interrupting everything, as usual. He spotted his mother, his wife, and Miles right away and strode over.

"Where?" he asked.

They all pointed to the back door. "By the firepit," said Myrtle helpfully.

Red gave her a look through narrowed eyes and headed off outside with a roll of yellow crime scene tape. After a couple of minutes, he came back in, giving a piercing whistle that cut through all the nervous chattering of the guests.

Red's voice was loud, but calm. "There's been a suspicious death on the premises. I need everyone to stay quiet and here on the grounds. Officers will be going around getting statements. This is all standard procedure. No one is allowed out the back doors." He gestured toward the back veranda and firepit.

He moved over to join them again. "Isabella?"

She nodded, looking tense.

"Sorry to have to see you under these circumstances. I'd like to speak with you first for a few minutes." He walked off to a corner of the room with Isabella, scattering a few guests as he did.

Soon, there were more officers on the scene. Then more as the state police started arriving. The officers busied themselves outside, although Myrtle noticed that one seemed to be stationed where he could keep guests from leaving.

Elaine sighed. "Poor Isabella. I feel so sorry for her. Here she is, trying to have a lovely event to get her winery off the ground, and then something like this happens." She lowered her voice. "Do you think this Ben Foster could have something to do with Gerald's death?"

"I have the feeling he's going to be a suspect, for sure, after Isabella fills Red in," said Myrtle. "After all, they apparently weren't getting along well. Maybe Ben blew up and did Gerald in."

They didn't wait long before Red was striding back over to speak with them again. His face was flushed almost as red as his hair. "Hi, Mama. Here we are again. I'm getting tired of this."

Myrtle gave him an indignant look. "I'm tiring of it too, Red. Perhaps you should consider more intense policing. It seems there are dead bodies fairly *littering* Bradley. Even at nice, respectable events like this one."

Red growled, "I'm used to poor Miles being dragged into these situations with you. But you rarely throw my wife into your shenanigans."

Elaine said, "Actually, this was *my* shenanigan. Remember my wine tasting hobby?"

Myrtle could tell he had conveniently forgotten about Elaine's latest hobby. It was a forgivable offense. Elaine's hobbies were legion and usually ended poorly. Then Red's gaze suddenly sharpened. "Where's Jack?" Red asked, head craning. He looked around him in horror as if the three-year-old might be tramping through his crime scene, toy trucks in hand.

"At a playdate, of course," said Elaine rather indignantly. "That's why we're all here, supporting Isabella."

"She's going to need support after this," said Red, shaking his head.

"It's murder," said Myrtle. "Strychnine, isn't it?"

Red leveled a look at his mother. "This is a subject that I don't want to be talking about with you. I'm not even sure why you know so much about poison. It's very unsettling hearing the word *strychnine* come out of an octogenarian's mouth."

Myrtle fingered the gift bag she was holding. The gnome was going to make a debut appearance with a cast of one-hundred in her front yard. Red was most annoying.

"Now please, let's get this over with so y'all can all go back to your respective homes. Miles, you got anything to offer on all this?"

Miles looked abashed. "I was asleep."

Red frowned. "Had some wine, did you?"

Miles now seemed even more uncomfortable. "A little, although I didn't even finish the tasting. I think it was more the stuffiness of the room with the fire running and all the people inside. But Myrtle is driving back, regardless, so don't worry about my intake."

Now *Red* was uncomfortable. Or, perhaps, alarmed. And Miles's words didn't have the soothing effect that Miles had intended. "Excuse me?"

"That was how we set it up," said Elaine. "I drove us over here. The arrangement was that Myrtle would drive us home. She barely drank a sip."

"I'm not worried about Mama driving drunk. I'm worried about Mama driving, *period*."

Myrtle glared at her son. "I beg your pardon! I'm an excellent driver. And I've become very accustomed to Elaine's minivan. I know where all the controls are."

Red closed his eyes momentarily. When he opened them, he said, "Okay. Let's go over the details of what happened so you can start out on your long journey home."

"Well, Miles was right. It *was* quite stuffy in here. It still is, despite all the police officers coming and going and opening the doors outside. Miles had nodded off in one of the armchairs in front of the fireplace. Elaine and I stepped out to look at the vineyard and get some fresh air. We settled at the firepit, and I noticed that the man across from us was Gerald Greystone. I also realized he was slumped rather oddly."

"Oddly, how?"

Myrtle said, "Just not in a natural position for someone who'd dropped off to sleep. Not like Miles, with his chin on his chest."

Miles blushed again at having been caught napping.

"You knew this Gerald?" asked Red. "I don't know if I recognize the name."

Elaine said, "Myrtle seems to know most people in town."

Myrtle beamed at her. "Well, first off, I knew Gerald's parents. They were older than me, but we were friendly. They're both gone now."

"Moved away?" asked Red, now jotting notes in a small notebook.

"Dead," said Myrtle.

"Ah."

"They were the ones who originally established the vineyard. They were lovely, hardworking people. They were fairly visionary, too. Few people at the time were thinking North Carolina could be remotely good for any sort of wine-making."

"Wait," said Red. "Gerald's parents owned *this* winery?"

"No, no." Myrtle gave her son an impatient look for not keeping up. "This winery is brand-new, Red. They owned the one next door to this one. Gerald, until today, still did."

"Did you teach Gerald?" asked Red. It was a fair question. Myrtle, at her advanced age, had taught many people of a certain age in Bradley, North Carolina before her long-ago retirement.

"He was too old for me to have taught. But I taught his ex-wife. Ramona. You remember who she was."

Red raised his eyebrows. "Yes, I do remember her. Wow. That was a significant age difference between the two of them."

"Yes. And they had a baby, nearly right after they married." Myrtle could tell that Red's attention was about to head solely to the ex-wife as a suspect. "Before you become too invested in Ramona's guilt, she lives in Canada now with her new husband. I'd imagine that would put her completely out of the picture for this crime."

Elaine said, "What did you make of Gerald, Myrtle? Since you knew him."

"Well, as I mentioned, I interviewed him a couple of years ago for a profile for the paper. I thought he was sort of smug, filled with his own self-importance. And something of a know-it-all. He was quite possibly also a control freak."

Red said, "That's quite a ruling on the man, Mama."

"It's well-deserved. I remembered asking him about his daughter and whether she was going to take over running the winery one day. A fair question, wouldn't you think? Gerald wasn't getting any younger, and he had a perfectly able daughter who could step in and take over his little empire. He was very condescending about her."

Red's gaze sharpened. "He was, was he?"

"That's correct. Julia, I think her name is. A lovely girl, from what I saw in the family photographs. Anyway, I thought Gerald's attitude was very odd. After all, his winery was basically a family enterprise, started by Gerald's parents." Then, suddenly, it occurred to Myrtle that she was giving far too much information away, having been lulled into doing so by everyone's interest in what she knew about Gerald's background. She decided to shut her mouth and tell her companions more about Gerald when Red and his little notebook weren't around. If Red wanted to solve the case, he was going to have to work for it.

Red seemed to sense Myrtle was now firmly opposed to being useful. He closed his notebook with a snap. "Okay. Now, I need you all to head home. Mama, obviously, I need you to stay focused and undistracted. It's not a short drive."

"For heaven's sake, Red! You realize I was driving twenty years before you were even born. That makes me an *expert* driver."

Red rolled his eyes. "I've heard that statement before. Just know that you've got precious cargo in the vehicle with you. I'll be checking on all of you to make sure you make it back safely."

Myrtle was about to give Red a piece of her mind when he slipped away, heading over to speak with one of the uniformed officers.

"Those gnomes are going to make an appearance as soon as I get home," muttered Myrtle as the three of them headed for the door.

Miles said, "You could call Dusty. He's probably still at your house, taking care of the yard."

"If he and Puddin ever made it over there, you mean." But it was a good idea. Myrtle carefully texted Dusty. He texted back. He wasn't delighted about the prospect of hauling gnomes out of the shed. Myrtle sweetened the pot by offering a little extra money. She needed to make a statement to Red that he couldn't denigrate her driving like that. She was an *excellent* driver.

They walked out into a blustery breeze and were all about to climb into the minivan again when they were waylaid by a middle-aged, grouchy looking man of average height with salt-and-pepper hair. He wore a knit hat that appeared homemade and a coat that seemed to have been hastily donned. "Hey there," he said in a gruff voice. "I was wondering if you could tell me what's going on at Serenity Springs."

Chapter Three

Myrtle frowned at him. "If you were there, you should know."

"I wasn't there. I enjoy going to Serenity Springs when it's actually serene, not when there's a party. I woke with a headache this morning. I live next door to Serenity Springs and adjacent to Greystone Grapes. I saw all the police cars pull up and just wanted to find out what happened." He stared at them with sharp, penetrating eyes under bushy eyebrows.

Myrtle snapped her fingers. "You're Frank Hayes, aren't you? I remember you. I believe you worked on my plumbing a year ago. Myrtle Clover. And this is Elaine Clover and Miles Bradford. How is your mother doing?"

She could hear Miles heave a sigh. He was clearly wanting to head back home and away from the winery. Now they were caught up in pleasantries with a looky-loo.

Frank said, "Oh, she's doing all right. She's in a home now. Greener Pastures."

Myrtle pursed her lips. She had lots to say about Greener Pastures. Miles cleared his throat pointedly, and she kept her thoughts to herself. "Well, isn't that nice," she said in a rather insincere voice. She frowned. "You know, I thought you lived on the other side of town, Frank."

"You have an excellent memory," he said. "I'm living in my mom's house now. She was okay with moving to the retirement home, but she wanted to keep the house. I sold mine and moved into hers. She had long-term care insurance, so we didn't have to sell her house to fund her stay at Greener Pastures." His gaze shifted to the winery again, as what looked like state police arrived. "I'm sorry, Miss Myrtle. Could you tell me what happened? I know you're Red's mom, so I figure you have a pretty good idea."

"I certainly do. Gerald Greystone died at Isabella's tasting. It appears to be a suspicious death."

Frank took a step back. "Died? What on earth happened? It wasn't the wine, was it?"

"It might have been something *in* the wine," said Myrtle circumspectly. "It's one of those things an autopsy will have to determine." She paused. "If you're living next door to Isabella's winery, that means you're also neighbors with Gerald. What did you make of him?"

Miles shifted uncomfortably on his feet, clearly wanting to leave. Elaine was already sitting in the back of the minivan, out of the wind, and scrolling on her phone.

Frank seemed taken aback by the question. "Gerald? Well, he and I got along fine as neighbors."

"When did you move into your mom's house?"

"Just in the last year. It hasn't been very long," said Frank. He was speaking carefully now, Myrtle noticed.

"How did your *mother* get along with Gerald then, since she seemed to have been his neighbor for far longer? When I met Gerald, he seemed like he could be a difficult man." This was a stretch, but Myrtle wanted to get an honest opinion. And getting honest opinions about a recently deceased murdered man could be difficult.

Frank said, "Oh, Mama was amazed by the changes at the winery in the years since Gerald took over the place from his folks. It grew so much and there were so many events and people and bands. People came from all over . . . like it was a destination."

"Gracious, that sounds like it might have been very loud. Crowds and bands? Did the noise ever bother her?"

Frank shrugged. "If it did, she simply took her hearing aids out."

Miles, having apparently resigned himself that he was going to be hanging out in the parking lot for a few more minutes, decided to interject. "Does the noise bother you, though?"

Frank looked a bit flushed at having Miles join the conversation. He might have forgotten he was even there. "It can bother me sometimes. But I thought it was very good for the local economy. People always came to Bradley for the lake, but then they didn't have anywhere else to really go, did they? I mean, there was the diner, of course. The winery has been here for a long time, but it wasn't as much of an attraction as it is now. So, yeah. I think the two wineries are good for Bradley."

Myrtle thought Frank hadn't entirely answered Miles's question. She also wondered if he was quite as cheerful about the bands and racket as he appeared. "Did you see Gerald much? I'd imagine you would, since you were neighbors. It's not as if there are many other people out here in the country."

"No, he was pretty busy." Frank's gaze flitted back to the winery. "What makes the cops think the death isn't natural? Was there something about Gerald's body?"

Myrtle didn't particularly feel like filling Frank in. There was something voyeuristic about his whole interest in Gerald's death that seemed to go beyond neighborly interest. She said, "I suppose there must have been. Perhaps you'll find out when Red talks to you."

Frank looked alarmed. "Talks to *me*? Why would he want to talk to me?"

"Why wouldn't he? You're the neighbor. You're the one who might provide some insight about Gerald. Insight is what solves cases." Myrtle regarded Frank thoughtfully. "As a neighbor, you might also be aware of who could possibly have wanted to kill Gerald. Was there anyone in particular who might have been upset with him?"

"Enough to kill him?" Frank seemed stunned by the idea. "I don't really know. I didn't really talk much to Gerald. We definitely weren't acquainted enough for him to tell me about people who disliked him."

Myrtle thought Frank was being deliberately obtuse. "But you might have heard other people give their thoughts on Gerald. Maybe they complained about him."

"Yeah, I know nothing about that." He stopped, looking again toward the winery. "This has got to be such a blow for Isabella. Here she is trying to get her new business off the ground and then this happens. I feel awful for her. Serenity Springs has only been open for a month and a half or so."

"How is *she* as a neighbor?"

"Much easier to get along with," admitted Frank. "Like I said before, I enjoy spending time in the tasting room when there aren't so many people here. I've had some great conversations with Isabella."

Myrtle wondered if Frank didn't have a little crush on his attractive neighbor. "How did Isabella get along with Gerald as her neighbor? I'd imagine Gerald would have been a great resource for her. A sounding board when she was starting out in the business."

Frank snorted at this. "Yes, he *could* have been. But from what I gathered from Isabella, he wasn't helpful at all. He thought of her as his competition."

Myrtle said, "Then it was rather odd that Gerald was here today at all." She didn't want to share that Isabella had invited Gerald to the wine tasting event. Although she thought it had been incredibly optimistic for Isabella to think Gerald would give the wines good reviews.

Frank gave a short laugh. "Why was he here today? Industrial espionage? Trying out the competition's goods? Only Gerald could answer that. But I bet it has something to do with his role as a wine critic. I doubt he was here to support Isabella. Don't get me wrong, I love Isabella."

Myrtle bet he did.

Frank continued, "But there was definitely some friction between her and Gerald. What a stroke of bad luck for him to die there. You're saying it's foul play, though. Isabella would never resort to any sort of violence at all. She's been totally dedicated to getting her business set up." He looked over again at the winery, regret on his features. "I sure hate this for her."

Myrtle said, "It's a terrible thing. But now, I'm afraid I've got to head back home. There's a playdate that's ending that I need to get my daughter-in-law back for." And a soap opera that was calling Myrtle's name again.

As they got into the minivan, Frank started heading back into the woods, apparently to his home, although it was impossible to see from there.

Miles said, "He's your plumber?"

"That's right. At least, he was for a short spate of time. Fortunately, since then, I've been free of plumbing issues. A good thing, since it usually costs a fortune just to have a plumber show up at your door." Myrtle started cautiously driving away from the winery at a stately ten miles an hour.

Miles didn't particularly want to distract Myrtle while she was concentrating on her driving. Elaine must not have wanted to either, because she was very quiet in the backseat. With Myrtle driving a top speed of twenty miles per hour, it took some time for them to make it back home. When they did, Myrtle carefully pulled into Elaine's driveway, putting the van in park. "There!" she said with satisfaction. "We're all good."

Elaine opened the sliding door to step out of the back of the minivan. "Thanks for driving, Myrtle. And I'm sorry for both of you. That definitely wasn't the morning I'd planned on us having. I'd envisioned us cozying up by the fire, sipping wines, sharing our thoughts, and then coming back home relaxed and revitalized."

"Gracious, no need to apologize! It was nothing to do with you and likely nothing to do with your friend Isabella." Myrtle was less convinced of the second part of the equation.

Miles gave Elaine a smile. "I enjoyed myself until the murder."

Elaine smiled back at him before her brow puckered. "You don't think Isabella is involved, do you? She's such a sweetheart. She's part of my women's coffee group, you know."

"I thought those were all moms," said Myrtle. "Does Isabella have kids?"

"No. And you're right about the coffee group, but we expanded to non-moms. Friends of friends and that sort of thing. Of course, Isabella hasn't been able to make it the last few weeks—too busy opening up the winery. I hope this doesn't put a major dent in her business. She was so excited about today."

Miles said, "I'm sure it will work out all right. It's not as if the winery is a dangerous spot."

"It was only dangerous for Gerald," said Myrtle dryly. "But I agree. I can't imagine people are going to hold a random incident against Isabella's business."

Elaine waved goodbye to them, thanked them again for coming, and set off to go inside. Myrtle said, "Want to come over? Watch the soap? See if Puddin actually accomplished anything?"

"Sure," said Miles. "It at least looks as if Dusty has been working. His truck's still here, too."

Myrtle gave a satisfied smile. "I noticed the gnomes when I drove in. Now my new one can join the clan." She took the vineyard gnome out of the shopping bag, carefully placing him among the others. She stepped back to review her handiwork before they walked inside. The door was unlocked. A game show was playing on the television.

Myrtle looked around, hands on her hips. "Where on earth is Puddin?"

"Maybe Dusty came without Puddin."

"He wouldn't dare," said Myrtle with narrowed eyes. "And Puddin has clearly been watching TV. For that matter, where's Dusty?"

The mystery of Dusty's whereabouts was soon solved when Miles discovered him sleeping in a folding chair in Myrtle's backyard.

"Puddin!" yelled Myrtle.

A muffled and sullen reply came from the back of the small house. Myrtle stomped over to her closed bedroom door. Pasha, Myrtle's feral cat, was sitting in front of the door, casually bathing herself.

Chapter Four

"What are you doing in there?" asked Myrtle.

"Get that witch-cat outta here, and I'll tell you."

Pasha gave Myrtle a feline smile. Myrtle reached down to rub her. "Darling Pasha. Want a can of tuna?" Tuna was a special treat, considering the fact that it often comprised a meal for Myrtle as well. But, considering Puddin was cowering behind a closed door, Myrtle figured Pasha likely deserved a reward of some kind.

Pasha happily padded behind her to the kitchen, where Myrtle dumped out the can of tuna on a plastic plate.

"The coast is clear," called Myrtle from the living room.

Miles watched with interest as Puddin cautiously left Myrtle's bedroom and joined them in the living room. Her pale, pasty face was full of indignation.

"Now, what happened?" asked Myrtle. "I can see that nothing has been accomplished here. And why is there such a sharp smell of lemon oil?"

Puddin snarled, "Thought it was floor cleaner."

"You cleaned my floors with lemon oil?" Myrtle gave Puddin a ferocious look. "No wonder the floors seemed slippery in the kitchen. You're going to have to mop again with the regular cleaner, or I'm going to break my neck. Unless that's part of your evil plan."

"I *got* no plan. Jest tryin' to do my job."

Myrtle said, "How did Pasha end up in the house? She certainly wasn't in here this morning when I left with Miles."

Puddin's mouth twisted resentfully. "Got in here, didn't she? When I was shaking out the feather duster outside."

Miles glanced around. "It looks as if the dusting has been done, Myrtle."

"Well, that's all that's been done."

"Nuh-uh!" said Puddin in a vicious tone. "Floors are done, too."

"They most certainly are not done. Weren't you even listening? They've all got to be mopped again to get the oil off. This is all most annoying, Puddin!"

Puddin said, "What's annoying is that witch-cat. She ran inside, then kept lookin' at me. Got closer and closer when I stopped for a second to take a break. Rest my back."

"Yes, I saw game shows were on. That must have been some break."

Puddin said defensively, "Didn't want to throw my back! That cat got closer and closer, so I had to shut myself in your room to get away."

Pasha padded back over to Myrtle. She shot Puddin a disdainful look that matched the one on Myrtle's face.

"Darling Pasha," said Myrtle, reaching down to rub the black cat. "She was simply trying to make sure you were working, not sitting around the living room."

"Can't work with that devil cat lookin' at me," insisted Puddin.

Myrtle heaved a sigh. "You're making life very difficult for me. I don't have time for this kind of foolishness, Puddin. I need to talk to Miles, then rest for a while with my soap opera. After that, I'm writing some articles for the paper. So you're going to have to figure out a way to handle this. Pasha lives here."

"Thought she lived outside," said Puddin, glaring at the cat. Pasha licked her paw to wash her face, totally unconcerned about Puddin's opinion of her.

"This is her inside home whenever she wants it. If she doesn't want to go out right now, I'm not going to make her. Miles, could you open the door for me?"

Miles complied. Pasha gazed at the front door with studied disinterest.

"There you go," said Myrtle as Miles closed the door back again. "She'd rather hang out with Miles and me for a while. Now carry on with the cleaning. Your poor husband is asleep outside, waiting for you."

"Didn't rescue me," muttered Puddin.

"I'm sure Dusty had no idea you were in extremis inside the house. He appeared to be snoring away."

Now Puddin was staring at the very shiny, very slippery floors with dissatisfaction. "Don't know how to clean this up."

"You'll have to figure it out."

Puddin scowled at the floors.

Miles helpfully looked up oil and floors on his phone. "If you scatter baking soda or salt on the floor and give it a few minutes, then you can vacuum or sweep the oil up. Then, I suppose, you'll want to mop it with floor cleaner.

Puddin stomped into the kitchen to find salt and baking soda.

"I expect you to bring me some supplies next time to replace what you're using," called Myrtle.

There was a muttered reply that was probably just as well Myrtle and Miles couldn't make out.

"Now we can proceed on with the soap opera and our regularly scheduled conversation," said Myrtle. "I can't believe I'm surrounded by such nonsense in my life, I honestly can't." She plopped down into her armchair and fiddled with the remote.

"On a completely different topic, what did you make of Frank?" asked Miles, perching on Myrtle's sofa.

Myrtle said, "Well, I thought he was very nosy about what was happening at the winery."

"Understandable, considering he was a neighbor. He had a vested interest in the area being safe."

Myrtle said, "Maybe. But there was still an element of prurience there that went beyond concern for his neighborhood. Frank was also clearly holding something back. Which, considering the circumstances, was probably smart. If he talked too much about the neighborly or unneighborly relationship between him and Gerald, he might quickly turn into a suspect."

"You think he and Gerald didn't get along?"

Myrtle said, "I'm pretty sure of it. I'd imagine Frank liked his peace and quiet. It sounds like Gerald's place was like a circus half the time. Maybe I can talk to Frank again later on, when I'm writing that piece about Isabella. Remind me to call Sloan later and tell him I have a couple of stories I'm working on."

Tomorrow's Promise started up its schmaltzy theme song swelling as images of the characters, all well-groomed young people, showed on the screen. When they'd last left off, the Thornfield's son, Gideon, had discovered a forbidden garden that was said to possess magical powers to alter destinies.

"Where are we with that garden storyline?" asked Miles. "I've lost track."

"Gideon is time-traveling. I think he was in the 1800s last episode. He's having a romance with Seraphina."

"A romance in the 1800s," said Miles. "Why don't I see a future for that romance?"

"You're right. He'll have to come back to the present day. The soap can't keep him in the 1800s forever. It wouldn't be sustainable."

Puddin plopped next to Miles on the sofa. "I wanna hear more about them twins that was separated at birth."

Myrtle gaped at Puddin. "What are you doing here? You're supposed to be cleaning up the mess you made with my floor!"

Puddin said sourly, "You heard him. I gotta let the oil soak up for a while. Gotta rest my back."

So for the next few minutes, Myrtle barely endured Puddin's inane questions about the complex storylines *Tomorrow's Promise* was doling out. Finally, the soaking time was up and Puddin stomped off to grapple with the floors again.

After the show was finished, Puddin was finished, too. Her stringy blonde hair was stuck to her flushed face, sweaty from exertion. She took her money from Myrtle, woke a startled

Dusty, and the two left in a cloud of exhaust and backfiring noises.

Miles said, "The more I think about poisoned wine, the ickier I feel."

"You were thinking about poison during the show? No wonder you're having a tough time keeping up with all the plot twists and turns."

"I can't help it. I think I want to head back home and take a shower," said Miles.

"I doubt that's going to help you with ingested poison."

"No, but it'll take care of the icky feeling," said Miles. He paused. "Hopefully, I'm not coming down with something. There were lots of people crammed into a small space. Maybe I should take some vitamin C or some zinc as a precaution."

"There hasn't been enough time to start having symptoms. Maybe you'll be sick tomorrow, though," said Myrtle helpfully. "Viruses take a while to incubate."

Miles looked even greener than he had when he was talking about the poison. "I'm heading out. See you later, Myrtle. Remember to call Sloan about the articles."

"Ah. Thanks for the reminder."

However, Myrtle realized she wasn't really in the mood to enter combat with Sloan. The problem there was that he always pushed back when it was time for her to become a crime reporter. It was most tiresome. Sloan had gone to school with Red, they were still friends of a sort, and Red basically forbade Sloan to allow his mother to interfere with his cases. Sloan always caved, but it was annoying to have to persuade him to give her the stories she wrote.

Myrtle decided she'd head outside for a short while and gather her strength for the irritating phone call ahead of her. It was a pretty day, and the wind seemed to have died down. Perhaps she should go out and see how her new gnome was fitting in.

Pasha looked up at her with interest as Myrtle stood by the front door. "Are you ready to go back outside, my darling?"

Pasha was. She padded quickly out the door, then slunk around the side of the house, instantly in hunting mode. Myrtle hoped it was one of the millions of squirrels and not one of the backyard birds she fed.

Myrtle headed out to her front yard. The imprudence of this action was forcefully brought to mind when her dreaded neighbor Erma Sherman appeared. Most of Myrtle's energy, she felt, was consumed by strategically avoiding Erma or escaping horrific conversations with her. She'd let her guard down and now Erma was upon her.

"Myrtle!" said Erma with delight, smiling her rodent-like smile. "I have news for you."

This was never a good thing. News from Erma usually meant excruciating details about her disgusting new medical condition. Myrtle gave her a wary look. "Do you?"

"Yes! I'm redoing my yard. Completely! I got a flyer from a yard service the other day. They did some kind of free evaluation."

One of those things where the company belittles your grass, then offers pricing options for solving the various lawn issues they identified. "I'm familiar with those," said Myrtle.

"Well, they told me I had all kinds of things wrong with my grass. Can you believe it? I mean, it's green, so I thought it was just fine."

One of the eternal mysteries to Myrtle was how Erma could be a paying member of garden club and not glean any helpful information about lawn care. "Well, you have dandelions, chickweed, crabgrass, clover, and goosegrass."

"See? That's exactly what I need to know. I need to know what's a weed and what's grass. Can you help me with that, Myrtle?"

Myrtle was now wanting to hit her head against a nearby tree. Or perhaps Erma's head, instead. All she'd wanted to do was come out and enjoy her gnomescape. And somehow, she'd gotten herself embroiled in Erma's yard project.

With the support of her cane, she leaned down as far as she could go.

"What're you doing?" asked Erma with concern. "Hey, I don't need you breaking a hip on my property."

Myrtle gritted her teeth and continued leaning over. She grasped a clump of fescue and pulled it up. "See this? This is grass. Anything that doesn't look like this needs to go."

Erma turned a hopeful gaze around her property. Then she frowned. "There isn't much that looks like that."

"Perhaps," said Myrtle cheerfully, "you should rip it all out and start over again from scratch."

"Why not? It's going to be an enormous project anyway. Might as well make it even bigger!"

Myrtle said, "An enormous project? Fixing your lawn?"

"Oh, the scope is going to be much larger than that. We're talking about fountains, landscaping. A water feature. Maybe even one of those garden mazes!"

Myrtle was stunned into silence, something that happened rarely, although it seemed to occur more often in Erma's presence. It suddenly occurred to her that the more time Erma spent outside with her pie in the sky yard project, the more she was going to endure run-ins with her.

"Anyway, I saw your gnomes out, Myrtle. What did Red do now?"

Myrtle found her voice again. "He was being obstreperous, as usual. About my driving."

Erma gave her that leering grin again. "You know Red just cares about you. You shouldn't be driving anyway, should you? You're practically ninety."

"I'm not," said Myrtle coldly. "I'm a card-carrying octogenarian. One that's just realized she has something important to address inside. I'll see you later, Erma."

"Enjoy your nap!" said Erma, giggling behind her, clearly incredulous that Myrtle's schedule would include anything important whatsoever.

Which was precisely when Pasha emerged from the shadows and headed directly for Erma. Erma let out a shriek. "Cat! Cat! I'm allergic! I'm allergic!"

The last Myrtle saw of Erma, she'd bolted for the safety of her home. A smile curled around Myrtle's mouth as Pasha turned and gave her a feline wink.

"Good girl," said Myrtle, stroking the black cat. Pasha bumped her head against Myrtle's hand before scampering off after some new prey. Myrtle, not wanting to risk another Erma encounter, headed back inside the house.

She still wasn't completely in the mood to tussle with Sloan over her newspaper article, especially since her recent bout of dealing with Erma's nonsense. But she picked up the phone with a sigh.

"Miss Myrtle!" said Sloan. It sounded as if he had dropped something. "What's up?"

Myrtle had taught Sloan high school English many years before. Whenever she called him, he appeared to revert to the classroom, apologizing for not having done his homework in time. "What's up is murder," said Myrtle coolly.

"Murder?" Sloan gave a startled laugh. "You didn't do Red in, did you, Miss Myrtle?"

"What? Certainly not! What a ridiculous idea, Sloan. There was a murder at Serenity Springs winery this morning. I was there, and I knew the victim. I'm going to write a story about it for the front page of the *Bugle* tomorrow."

Sloan appeared to be trying to wrap his head around all the information Myrtle had just presented him with. "Who was the victim?"

"Gerald Greystone. You'll remember I interviewed him some time ago for a profile piece we did on him."

Sloan said slowly, "Oh, right. I do recall that. And he was murdered?" His voice was sounding even more nervous than it had before.

"That's correct. At the winery. This morning. I'm writing a story on it." Myrtle carefully repeated all the information she'd already provided to Sloan. She was wondering if his beer drinking had perhaps started earlier in the day than it ordinarily did.

"Okay," said Sloan, obviously trying to think of a way out of having Myrtle write a crime story. "How about if you do a profile on the Serenity Springs winery instead? Maybe we can get them to advertise. It's a new place and they'll be looking for some positive coverage. I'll handle the story about Gerald's murder."

"I'm a step ahead of you. I've already told the owner that I'll write a puff piece on her and the winery. But I'm writing that article on the murder. I've already started," said Myrtle, crossing her fingers behind her back at the lie.

Sloan blew out a sigh. "Red's not going to like it."

"Red's not going to like anything I do. I might as well just write it."

Perhaps sensing that he was going to get nowhere with persuading Myrtle to back off the story, Sloan finally capitulated. "Okay, okay. Go ahead and tackle it, Miss Myrtle. You always do a fine job, anyway."

Myrtle glowed at the praise, although she considered it well-deserved. "Excellent. I'll be sure to bring you something the next time I see you. Some home-baked brownies, perhaps."

Sloan hastily said, "That won't be necessary, Miss Myrtle. Just worry about your article. See you soon." And he swiftly hung up.

Chapter Five

The rest of the day was quite a bit quieter than the first part. Myrtle wrote and submitted the story. Pasha decided to come back in to spend more time with Myrtle as she knocked out a crossword from her puzzle book. She ended up turning in fairly early, but spent far too much time tossing around uncomfortably, trying to sleep. Giving up around four, Myrtle started her Sunday. As soon as the paper was delivered, she checked to make sure her story was front and center. It was. She smiled. More ammunition to irritate Red with.

Her Sunday morning was quiet. She'd texted Miles to see if he wanted to come over for breakfast, but he didn't respond. Miles must have slept in after his harrowing morning yesterday. Myrtle filled her time with watching a nature documentary, completing a Sudoku, and peering out the window to see what Erma was doing in her yard.

After lunch, Myrtle went to the library, which opened at noon on Sundays. She had a book to return. And she knew she had an upcoming book club, which made her shudder. She'd take a look at the selection for the month and see if it appealed at all. Myrtle had begun thinking that perhaps book club should be divested of its name. Since it seemed to have very little to do with books and much more to do with gossip and eating, it should be called social hour, instead. The book selections were pitiful and the discussions on the thin plots the books offered were just as pathetic. Perhaps she'd find a better book for the group for next month's event. Then she remembered the club was doing some sort of theme for the following month. Myrtle grimaced.

Walking in through the library doors, however, Myrtle felt better. There was something about being surrounded by books that lifted her spirits. There were also some darling little children with their moms who were getting board books and the like. She decided she'd pick up a few books for Jack while she was there, too. Although Jack, considering his intellect, was far beyond board books.

She pulled out some old favorites from the children's section for her grandson. *Mike Mulligan and His Steam Shovel, The Story of Ferdinand,* and *Make Way for Ducklings* were cradled in her arm as she leaned on her cane with the other. Somewhat off-balance, she made a bit of a stumble on her way to the mystery section across the way. A young man reached out and grabbed her arm.

"Heavens," said Myrtle. "Thank you."

"It's no problem at all," said the young man, smiling at her. "I'm using this study table . . . do you want to set your books down on it while you look for others?"

Myrtle beamed at him. "Well, aren't you nice? Yes, I'll take you up on that. If I didn't have this cane, I'd be able to carry more. Silly of me not to bring a bag."

"I'm sure they probably have a plastic bag behind the circulation desk that you could use when you're ready to leave."

"An excellent suggestion." She paused. "Pardon me for being nosy, but are you perhaps Ben Foster? Gerald Greystone's manager; is that right?" During Myrtle's peaceful Sunday morning, she'd taken the time to look up a few people online. Ben was one of them. Isabella and Frank were the others.

Ben was clearly surprised. "Yes, I am. I'm sorry—do I know you?"

"Oh, no apologies needed. I sort of blend into the background. I'm Myrtle Clover. I was at Serenity Springs yesterday and found poor Gerald. I wrote a profile on him a little while back for the newspaper."

Ben still looked uncertain as to why this very elderly lady would know who he was. But he moved on to the fact that she'd discovered his murdered boss. "That must have been very upsetting."

Myrtle had grown accustomed to people thinking it was upsetting when she found a body. She simply nodded. "I understand you're some sort of vineyard wunderkind. At least, that's what Isabella was saying."

Ben gave a small laugh. "I think Isabella was flattering me. I do what I can." He paused. "Hey, do you mind taking a seat with me for a few minutes? I've been dying for information about what happened, but I can't seem to find any."

Myrtle supposed that someone his age didn't read the newspaper. It was a pity. He'd have been able to have many of his questions answered, if he had. "Of course. I'll be happy to tell you what I know."

She settled down at the small table with him. Ben was an earnest-looking young man of about thirty with blond hair, blue eyes, and something of a shy manner. She smiled at him. "Wunderkind was definitely the right word. If you'll excuse me for saying so, you seem very young to be in charge of a large production like Gerald's vineyard."

He grinned back at her. "I agree with you. I definitely appreciated Gerald putting his trust in me. I went to Clemson for a horticulture degree, then had some experience during the summers working in vineyards. But yes, I think I'm probably pretty young compared to most vineyard managers." He leaned forward over the table, making sure no one was within earshot. "I was very sorry to hear about Gerald. I've been here trying to kill time while the cops are over at Greystone Grapes."

"They're searching the place, I'm guessing," said Myrtle. "Looking for any indication of why Gerald's life might have been taken."

"That's right. Of course, they didn't tell me anything. I was hoping you could fill me in."

Myrtle said, "I'd be happy to. And I wonder if you might answer a few questions for me, as well. I work for the local paper, and I'm the one reporting on the crime."

Ben shifted a little nervously. "Would it be off the record?"

"If you'd like it to be. I'm just trying to get some background information on Gerald and the winery." Myrtle rummaged in her tremendous purse to find a small notebook and a pen hoping to make it all look very official. "Just for my benefit, you know. Off the record, like we said."

Once she was all set up, she launched into it. "The room had gotten stuffy, so I stepped outside with my daughter-in-law. We sat over by the firepit so we'd stay warm, but still enjoy the breeze. I saw a *very* relaxed gentleman sitting across from me."

"He was still alive?" asked Ben, swallowing.

"No, I'm afraid not. That's the reason I was so curious about the way he was slumped. It didn't seem like a natural angle in which to sleep. I also recognized the figure as Gerald. I reached over to shake his shoulder and realized he was gone." Myrtle phrased it all very delicately, since she wasn't sure if Ben had been close to Gerald. Isabella had said that Ben and Gerald had differences of opinion regarding the running of Greystone Grapes. But that didn't mean Ben hadn't been fond of Gerald.

In a quiet voice, Ben asked, "Could you tell what happened? Could you tell it wasn't a natural death?"

Myrtle paused. She wasn't at all sure that Red or the state police wanted information about the cause of death spread around. However, considering how quickly rumors and gossip flitted around Bradley, she was also certain that word had likely gotten out. She decided not to mention strychnine, specifically.

"It certainly looked like he'd been poisoned," said Myrtle carefully.

Ben's eyes grew wide. "Poison in his food? Or in his drink?"

"I didn't see any evidence of food nearby. He did have a glass of wine in front of him."

Ben shook his head. "The poor guy. That's awful."

There was a long pause where Ben seemed to try to absorb the information. Myrtle, however, wanted to keep him talking. Perhaps some straightforward questions about his work would be the best way to facilitate that. She cleared her throat. "I'm afraid I don't know very much about the wine business. What sorts of things are you usually tasked with?"

Ben perked up then, and he got a sparkle in his eyes. He was clearly a guy who loved his job. "Oh, lots of different things, mostly depending on the time of year. I help with overseeing the harvests, of course. I also manage the fermentation, aging, and bottling practices."

"That all sounds very scientific," said Myrtle with some surprise. She hadn't put a lot of thought into how grapes turned into wine.

Ben bobbed his head. "There's definitely a chemical aspect to winemaking. But I do less-scientific stuff, too, like overseeing vineyard maintenance—pruning, pest control, things like that."

"You probably have a fair number of workers to manage, I'd imagine."

"That's correct. Then there are office-related types of things that I handle, including inventory, marketing and promotion, and event coordination."

"Mercy!" said Myrtle. "Did you ever sleep?"

"Sometimes," said Ben with a laugh. "I love my job, though, so I just keep on plugging."

"Do you also help with the books? The financial side of things?"

Ben said, "At first, Gerald was handling more of that. As time went on, though, he started delegating more and more of that stuff to me, too." He shifted in his seat, looking as if he wanted to talk about the murder again. "How was Isabella's event going? Before the murder, I mean."

"It seemed very successful. There were far more people there than I'd thought there would be. Everyone appeared to be having a good time."

Ben said, "That's good. I hope this incident hasn't messed anything up for her. I really want her to succeed."

"You don't think of Isabella as competition?"

Ben shook his head. "No. I think of her as part of the community of wine growers."

Myrtle remembered Isabella saying how helpful Ben had been in giving her advice. "I'm surprised you weren't over at Serenity Springs yesterday."

Ben looked rueful. "Gerald would have considered it industrial espionage." He chuckled. "Or maybe I should say *agricultural* espionage. Anyway, Gerald wouldn't have wanted me there."

"But Gerald was there himself," pointed out Myrtle.

"Yes, but he wasn't going to be disclosing anything about our grapes or process. He was just there to sample Isabella's wines."

"Was he?" asked Myrtle. "I know Gerald was quite the wine critic. Might he have been there to *write* about Serenity Springs?"

"It's possible," admitted Ben. "I doubt the reviews would have been glowing, no matter how great the wines were."

"Because Gerald was so competitive."

"That's right. I don't think he'd have slammed Isabella's wines, but he sure wouldn't have raved over them," said Ben.

"That's quite a conflict of interest there. If Gerald wasn't going to be objective, he shouldn't have been planning to review the wines." She paused. "Have the police spoken with you about the murder?"

"Yes," said Ben, looking a little sick at the thought. "But they didn't disclose any information about Gerald's death. I couldn't believe it when they told me the news. All they told me was that he was dead, then they hit me with a barrage of questions about Gerald and my thoughts on him."

Myrtle raised her eyebrows. "Did you get the impression they might have considered you a suspect?"

Ben hastily looked around them as if library patrons might be horning in on their conversation. But everyone was in their own little world and not at all interested in theirs. "I did. Maybe they're thinking everybody is a suspect right now, though. I don't know. I've never even spoken to a police officer before. It freaked me out. They were asking where I was when Gerald died."

"Did you have any sort of alibi to give them?"

"I wish. But I was at work in the office at the winery. I was knocking out some of the budgeting stuff. No one saw me there, either. The workers were out in the vineyard, so no one witnessed me there."

Myrtle asked, "What was it like working with Gerald? Was he a good employer?"

Ben looked conflicted. "Well, I didn't harbor any bad feelings toward the guy."

"But?"

Ben said, "But he could be a difficult person to work around. He was a real perfectionist. Not only that, but he was a person who had lots of big ideas and wanted to implement them." He rubbed his forehead. "It's a real shame somebody ended his life before he could make all those ideas into reality."

There was something almost practiced in the way Ben spoke about Gerald. Maybe he'd been prepared to be peppered with questions by everybody in town. She wondered what he really felt about his boss. "What were some of Gerald's ideas for the vineyard? It sounds as if he was something of a visionary."

"He was, in a way," said Ben. He looked a little reluctant to go into his ideas. Myrtle could tell by his expression that he didn't think much about Gerald's plans.

To coax more out of him, Myrtle said, "One neighbor mentioned Gerald was having lots of events. Music and so forth. Were Gerald's ideas about furthering those kinds of activities? Making the events bigger?"

Ben nodded. "That was part of it." He stopped short, as if warring with himself over what to say. Finally, his desire to talk won out over being more circumspect. "There was nothing really wrong with Gerald's plans. It's just that he and I had different visions for Greystone Grapes. I was worried that the integrity of the vineyard was going to be compromised."

That seemed rather an extreme reaction to Myrtle, but she nodded as if she agreed. "You thought he was putting too much time and money into things that weren't related to the grapes, I'm guessing?"

Ben looked relieved that she seemed to catch on. "That's right," he said eagerly. "He was channeling a lot of funds into things that weren't the core of his business. We used to have events, of course, but they were cozy. We were throwing these large, kind of impersonal events. Greystone Grapes was in danger of losing its essence and identity."

"Were Gerald's ideas going to take the vineyard in a very commercial direction?"

Ben nodded. "Exactly. He was prioritizing profit over producing exceptional, small-batch wines. We were having creative differences. It's like having too many cooks in the kitchen. Gerald had been the winemaker before he handed the reins over to me. But he was still around, always thinking about the wine. It was as if he were looking over my shoulder. But I was more intent on the wine quality than he was. That's my opinion, of course."

It might have been Ben's opinion, but she could tell by his expression that he was convinced it was the truth. Myrtle thought this through. "Was Gerald producing enough wine to take the business in that commercial direction you mentioned?"

"Not at all. He wanted to ramp up production. Quantity over quality. I was worried the vineyard's tradition of exceptional wines was going to be compromised by mass production."

"Hm," said Myrtle. "It sounds like you were really looking out for the vineyard's reputation."

That clearly pleased Ben. "I was trying to," he said eagerly. "I just didn't think we should mess with success. Gerald was getting interested in taking more risks. I thought we should be careful with how we proceeded."

"What kinds of risks?" asked Myrtle. Her imagination was going wild, trying to picture what risky behavior Gerald might have encouraged.

But it was something quite a bit more sedate than Myrtle had imagined. Ben said in a bit of a scornful tone, "He was interested in new grape varietals instead of time-tested options. Also, I had some sustainability concerns. Gerald was pushing overuse of pesticides and herbicides, which could lead to soil and water pollution. Those could easily harm local ecosystems, along with the chemical fertilizers he was pushing."

Ben stopped with a start when his phone started ringing. Myrtle looked over and could see the name *Julia Greystone* pop up. As she recalled, that was the name of Gerald's grown daughter.

Ben turned red and flustered when he answered the phone. "Yes, hi! Julia? It's Ben." He grimaced at his awkwardness. He clearly didn't need to identify himself if she was the one who'd called him. He looked so miserable that Myrtle slid a peppermint candy across to him. He gave her a weak smile.

"Sure, of course. I'd be happy to speak to you." He grimaced again. "I mean, I'm very sorry about your dad. Naturally, you'd like to talk it over. Anytime. Okay. Thanks."

He hung up, looking even pinker than he had when he'd first answered the brief call. "That was Julia Greystone. She wants to meet up to talk about what happened to Gerald. Or maybe talk about what's going to happen with the business."

"What *is* going to happen to the business?"

Ben shook his head. "No idea. Maybe Julia knows." His eyes took on a wistful expression.

"I'd imagine Julia would be the heir, wouldn't she?" asked Myrtle, frowning. "I don't recall Gerald mentioning any other children."

"No, she's the only child."

"And Gerald was divorced, I believe," added Myrtle.

"That's right. Although he was seeing someone." A look of distaste passed across Ben's very readable face.

"Someone objectionable?"

Ben said slowly, "I wouldn't necessarily say that. The only thing that I didn't care for is that she seemed to always put Gerald in a terrible mood. And Gerald wasn't the kind of person who could shake off a mood like that. He'd pass it along to other people—being cranky with the vineyard workers, his daughter, or me." He shrugged. "It looked like they had a terrible relationship. Of course, I was looking at it from the outside, so who am I to say?"

"What was his girlfriend's name?"

"Liv. Liv Anderson." Ben suddenly looked discomfited. "It didn't even occur to me to notify her about Gerald's death. I've been working on statements for our social media, but I didn't think about Liv."

"I wouldn't worry about it. The police almost certainly have already found out about her and let her know."

Ben shifted in his chair. "I guess so. It would have been hard for her *not* to know what was going on, considering the police were crawling all over the winery."

Myrtle said, "I'm curious about the set-up over there. Am I to understand that Gerald lived on the site? And that you do, too?"

Ben nodded. "Yes, ma'am. That's how Gerald sweetened the pot for me to take the job. And Liv had moved in with Gerald, too. It's a big operation over there. There's a small cottage on the grounds where I live. Great views, all the amenities, rent-free."

Myrtle quirked an eyebrow. "And probably no boundaries between work and your personal life."

Ben's grin grew crooked. "Not a problem. I don't *have* a personal life. Gerald and Liv were in the big house that's behind the vineyard." He paused. "It must have been terrible for Liv to discover police searching through the house and being told that way. I'm sure she was upset, even though their relationship seemed to be crummy."

"Why did Liv put Gerald in a bad mood all the time?"

Ben sighed. "Well, she seemed convinced he was constantly having affairs with other women."

"Was he?"

"I don't think so," said Ben. "At least, not that I could tell." He paused. "I should probably get back and see if the cops will let me in." He looked at Myrtle's picture books. "Why don't I hold these for you while you find the other books you were going to check out?"

She beamed at him. "Well, aren't you a nice young man? Thank you. I just wanted to pick up a couple of things."

Myrtle could dredge up the theme she was supposed to be following for the next month's book club. It was *guilty pleasures*. Myrtle made a face. The members were all to share what their guilty pleasure reads were and then vote on the winner. She was sure the club expected some sort of lurid tale for that selection. She picked up a Jane Austen book. A bit of light reading to Myrtle's way of thinking. Then she hastily stopped by another stack of books, consulting her phone to see what the current month's selection was. As she'd expected, it was complete tripe. She snorted and left it on the shelf, hurrying back to Ben Foster, who was patiently waiting while holding the stack of children's books. When he spotted her, he took the Austen book from her and slid all the books onto the circulation desk. "There you are," he said. "Good talking to you."

"Hope things look up for you soon," said Myrtle.

She ordinarily checked out her own books, but since she was hoping to persuade the library to part with a plastic bag for her return walk home, she had the librarian do it. "Do you have a plastic grocery bag?" asked Myrtle in her most polite manner. She affected a frail look. At nearly six feet, it was a difficult thing to accomplish. "It's a little tricky to hold the books and my cane at the same time."

The librarian said, "Oh my goodness, of course it would be! Let's get you set up with one of the library's tote bags."

Never one to embrace unexpected expenses, Myrtle said, "How much are those?"

The librarian made a dismissive gesture with one hand. "It's our pleasure. I see you've been a library patron for . . ." The librarian peered at the computer, pushing her glasses up with one hand. "Gracious. For the last seventy-eight years?"

"That seems about right."

"Well, I think that your loyalty deserves a free tote bag," said the librarian, pulling it off of a shelf behind the circulation counter. The bag had a picture of books on it and said: *Book Lovers: Turning Pages and Turning Heads.*

"Thank you," said Myrtle, pleased.

She was about to leave the library with her books and new tote bag when she heard her name called. Myrtle nearly pretended she couldn't hear it, because she recognized the voice. Tippy. And her voice had sounded brisk. That was Project Tippy. And Myrtle didn't particularly want to be saddled with a project.

Myrtle took a step toward the sliding doors, but Tippy was suddenly right there, well-heeled as always, with white slacks and a blue silk blouse. Her carefully arranged blonde coif didn't have a hair out of place. "Myrtle," she said with a smile. "Glad I could catch you."

"You must be here getting the book club selection," said Myrtle.

"No, I'm volunteering with the Friends of the Library."

Myrtle gave her a tight smile. Of course Tippy was. And soon, if Tippy had her way, she'd ensure Myrtle was volunteering for something, too. Or volun-told, as the case might be.

"I was going to call you later today," said Tippy. "The church is in dire need of someone to help with sorting clothes at the clothes closet. For those in need."

The last words were said with emphasis. Myrtle slumped. It would sound churlish for her to decline.

"It sounds like a fairly active role," said Myrtle slowly. "Standing, sorting, bagging?"

"Not for you. We'll set you up in a comfy chair. You'll just be sorting and someone else will be bagging."

Myrtle sighed. She knew when she was hooked. "Yes, that sounds fine. When do you need me to help out?"

"Right now would be perfect," said Tippy with a smile. "I've just finished with my work here. I can drive us over to the church, and we'll work side by side."

"Lovely," said Myrtle.

And so Myrtle climbed into the leather interior of Tippy's very expensive, very large car, setting her tote bag of books on the floorboard.

Chapter Six

Tippy set off toward the church. "I didn't see you in the sanctuary this morning," she said, looking sideways at Myrtle.

"Hmm? Oh. No, I wasn't able to make it this morning."

Tippy said, "Did you make it to Sunday school?"

"No, I didn't make that, either." Myrtle was feeling sulky now. She really should have bolted from the library when Tippy was calling to her.

"Well, you missed a wonderful sermon this morning. If you'd like me to pick you up on Sundays, I'd be more than happy to." Tippy's eyes lit up at the thought of Myrtle becoming her new project.

"That won't be necessary," said Myrtle quickly. "I'm more inclined to the Emily Dickinson school of thought, regarding the Sabbath."

Tippy frowned. "Emily Dickinson? Was she a minister?"

Myrtle was taken aback. Tippy's brain must have gotten polluted by too many vapid book club books. "No, a famous poet from the 19th century."

"Oh." Tippy's voice now indicated she was losing interest in the conversation.

"Emily wrote about how she was able to worship God at home, with the wonders of nature around her," said Myrtle pointedly.

"I see," said Tippy. "So you spend Sunday mornings outside?"

She had her there. Myrtle hesitated and said, "I keep the windows open. I'm quite a bit more elderly than Emily was at the time."

To Myrtle's relief, Tippy was inclined to change the subject. "I heard you were at Serenity Springs yesterday for that wine tasting."

"Yes. With Elaine and Miles. I suppose you heard what happened."

Tippy said, "I read your article in the paper. Such a shame. A terrible end to an intelligent and ambitious man."

"You knew Gerald?"

"Not very well. I'd met him once or twice. But as a member of the town council, I know how successful his business was and how vital to the local economy." She frowned as she pulled into the church parking lot. "I worry about the impact of the murder on Isabella's business, too. Perhaps she'll need to advertise."

"I'm actually interviewing her for a profile in the paper," said Myrtle.

"Oh, that sounds like a wonderful idea. That makes me feel better about her prospects."

"What did you make of Gerald?" asked Myrtle.

Tippy paused. "What did *you* make of him? It sounds as if you knew him, too."

"Only a little. My impression of him had been generally positive." Although Myrtle was now starting to second-guess that opinion.

"Hmm. Yes." Tippy hesitated, perhaps not wanting to speak ill of the dead. She carefully parked her luxury car in a spot.

"You felt differently?"

Tippy said slowly, "Well, I certainly respected his business acumen and his entrepreneurial spirit. Although I didn't think much of the way he treated other people."

"Surely, he treated the guests at Greystone Grapes well."

"Of course. At least, I'm sure he did. But I know for a fact that he's never been kind to his family. I was acquainted with his ex-wife," said Tippy.

"Ramona, yes. She lives in Canada, I believe."

"That's right," said Tippy. "I'm afraid Ramona's life with Gerald was miserable. He was a very exacting, critical person. From what she told me, he also expected their daughter, Julia, to be a mini-adult, even when she was very small."

Myrtle shook her head. "Well, he sounds horrid. Something like a control freak. Although, it seems odd that he stepped back and hired a manager and winemaker to run his business for him."

"Ben Foster," said Tippy, nodding. "I saw him at the library before I spotted you. Such a nice young man. He seems to be quite the reader. When I mentioned Friends of the Library, he appeared to be very interested in volunteering."

Myrtle felt this was said in something of a pointed manner. "Did Ben talk about working for Gerald at all?"

Tippy said, "He mostly framed it in positive terms. But he told me Gerald was quite a taskmaster. Ben lives on site and Gerald seemed to feel like that made it okay for Ben to work around the clock. Gerald apparently had an erratic sleep schedule and would text or call Ben in the middle of the night when things occurred to him."

"Awful!" said Myrtle with condemnation, conveniently forgetting the many times her own insomnia had propelled her to show up at Miles's doorstep for coffee and conversation.

Tippy said, "Yes. Of course, Ben is a young person, so he's perhaps better-equipped to handle it than most. Even so, it went far and beyond the call of duty."

Myrtle said, "How well do you know Isabella?" Tippy knew everyone, of course, but there were different degrees of acquaintance.

"Fairly well," said Tippy with a shrug. She opened the car door pointedly, and Myrtle reluctantly followed her toward the church. "She's clearly very different from Gerald, but just as driven, don't you think?"

"Driven to pursue success?"

Tippy said, "Exactly. But also just driven in general. She seems to have a lot of energy, wouldn't you say? She's the kind of person who has a hard time sitting still. I suspect she multitasks." Tippy's tone spoke volumes.

"You're not fond of multitasking?"

Tippy held the door leading into the church open for Myrtle and again, she reluctantly followed. "Multitasking simply doesn't work. There have been multiple studies showing that. Humans just aren't programmed that way. Believe me, if I thought there was a method to make me more productive, then I would adopt it."

Myrtle had no doubt of that. Tippy was the personification of productivity. But she didn't believe in shortcuts, and she always wanted to do a good job at everything she took on.

"But despite my misgivings about Isabella's attempts at multitasking, it seemed she was doing an excellent job at Serenity Springs. Even more important, her staff seemed to love her."

Myrtle said, "As opposed to Gerald's staff?"

"Correct." Tippy walked down a narrow corridor near the church office and into what seemed like a large closet. The rather claustrophobic space was filled with black trash bags.

"Heavens," said Myrtle.

Tippy briskly pulled up a chair and pointed to it. "Yes. You can see why I said this was an all-hands-on-deck situation. These clothes need sorting by type and by size. Then they'll head off to the clothing closet for anyone who needs them. We're going into the winter, and I can't stand the thought that clothes that could be useful are sitting here in bags at the church."

Myrtle wisely kept her mouth shut and started sorting. Tippy was clearly on a tear and if she didn't watch it, Myrtle might end up signed up for clothes sorting for the foreseeable future.

Tippy was just as type-A and exacting about the process as she'd reported Gerald to be about his vineyard. She made sure that Myrtle didn't put track pants in the same pile as denim, although in Myrtle's mind, they should both be in the "casual pants" category. She was also critical of Myrtle's decision to put tank tops in with underwear.

"Those are casual tops," said Tippy firmly.

Myrtle frowned at them. "Are you sure? They seem rather revealing." Myrtle held up one of the offending garments.

"Young people consider those to be tops."

Myrtle continued on with her work, ready for her clash with the generation gap to be over. Finally, they were through. It took them two hours to sort the clothes. Tippy looked around the room with satisfaction. "Well done."

Tippy still looked fresh as a daisy, despite just having volunteered for both Friends of the Library and the clothes closet. Myrtle, on the other hand, was feeling like she'd been run over by a truck. Perhaps it was the repetitive motion of the sorting. Or perhaps it was being stuck with Tippy in a confined space for far too long of a time.

Tippy quickly noticed that Myrtle seemed drained. "Let's take you home. You have something healthy to eat at home, don't you?"

Myrtle had to consider this. She remembered too late that she'd planned on hitting the grocery store that afternoon. "Eggs. They're healthy."

Tippy pursed her lips, clearly not impressed by Myrtle's food inventory. "I think I should pay for supper for you."

Myrtle was alarmed at the thought of spending more time with Tippy after an already Tippy-intensive afternoon. "I'll be fine, Tippy. I'd like to get back home instead of going to a restaurant."

"No restaurant required. The Piggly Wiggly has a nice selection of ready-to-eat deli meals. We'll slide by there and I'll run in and grab one for you."

Myrtle had, occasionally, seen those available at the store. However, they'd always seemed out of line with her budget. Although it irked her a bit to have Tippy take her dinner on as a project, she had to admit to some curiosity about the ready-made meals. "Thank you," she said, as graciously as she could muster.

Tippy led the way out of the large closet room and down the narrow corridor again. "Mushroom and spinach stuffed chicken breast? Or teriyaki salmon with brown rice?"

Myrtle quirked a brow. Clearly, Ms. Perfect had availed herself of the ready-made meals herself from time to time. "Teriyaki salmon sounds good."

"Excellent choice," said Tippy.

They were about to head out to the parking lot from the church vestibule when they literally ran into a young woman with long, dark hair and a surprising October suntan.

"I'm so sorry," said the young woman, reaching out to steady Tippy and Myrtle. The woman looked familiar to Myrtle, but she couldn't quite place her.

Tippy, naturally, could. "Julia! Oh, gracious. I'm so terribly sorry about your father." She turned to Myrtle. "This is Myrtle Clover."

"Of course. Good to see you again, Miss Myrtle."

Myrtle's memory jogged. The young woman was Julia Greystone, Gerald's daughter. She'd thought that she'd only seen her in a photo, but now she remembered she'd briefly met her those years ago when she'd been leaving her interview with Gerald. "It's a pleasure to see you again, my dear. Although I'm so sorry for the circumstances. You're at the church to plan the service?"

She nodded, seeming very composed. Myrtle, who was a great fan of composure, was relieved. However, just in case things took a turn, she knew she had a fresh packet of tissues in her large purse. Julia said, "That's right. It's tomorrow, actually. The minister gave me a hand with the planning. He was very helpful—a good thing, because I feel like I don't really have my head screwed on right just now."

"Of course you don't," said Tippy briskly. "What a horrible last two days it's been for you."

Julia looked concerned. "Do you think it's all right to go ahead and hold a memorial service? People won't think it's too rushed? It's just that I felt some closure might be really helpful for me."

Tippy said, "They certainly won't think it's too rushed." Tippy's tone boded ill for anyone who dared to voice an opinion to that effect.

Myrtle said, "It's always been standard procedure in the South to hold services after two or three days." She tactfully didn't say that the original reason for this was that the South was a hot place with little air conditioning until later in the twentieth century.

Julia gave them both a smile. "Thanks. I'll feel better going forward, then. My dad's body hasn't been released by the police yet, and when he is, he'll be cremated. That was always his wish." She sighed. "It's all been very overwhelming. One minute, Dad was there, larger than life. The next, he was gone. It's like there was no transition at all."

She looked over at Myrtle and said hesitantly, "I don't suppose you've heard anything at all from Red about how the investigation is progressing?"

"Unfortunately, my son doesn't talk about his cases." Myrtle sourly reflected that it would be more accurate to say that whenever Red *did* talk to her, it was to fuss at her about something.

Julia said, "I'm just nervous that the police think I had something to do with Dad's death."

"I'm sure they don't," said Tippy in a soothing voice.

Myrtle didn't offer any reassurances. She was fairly certain that Julia, as heir to Greystone Grapes, would be high on the list of suspects.

Chapter Seven

Tippy said, "Maybe we should sit down somewhere."

Myrtle thought Tippy was saying this because of Julia, but it was soon clear by her expression that she thought Myrtle might tip over in exhaustion after her clothing sorting. With irritation, Myrtle followed Tippy and Julia to the church parlor, thumping her cane as she walked. It was a stuffy room with lots of toile and old wood. They all sat down in the rather prissy-looking armchairs. Tippy shut the door firmly behind them, saying, "We don't want a Bible study interfering."

Julia looked down at her hands for a few moments, as if not sure where to start.

Myrtle said, "Why were you concerned that Red thinks you had something to do with your father's death?"

Tippy shot Myrtle a look.

Julia said, "Mainly because Dad and I didn't always get along. And because I don't have an alibi for his death."

"I'm sure you're not the only one without an alibi," said Myrtle. "It was a Saturday morning. It's not as if people were at work with plenty of witnesses around."

This made Julia relax a little. "That's true. I was just starting out on a quiet weekend at home."

"And you don't live at Greystone Grapes, do you?" asked Myrtle.

"No. I moved out years ago," said Julia.

"And you work at the winery?" asked Myrtle. She knew full well that Gerald hadn't involved Julia in the family business, but she wanted to see what Julia would say.

Julia looked down at her hands again. "No. It would be nice to say that I work in the wine industry, but I'm actually a dog groomer. Well, some cats too, but usually just dogs." She smiled. "I actually really enjoy it."

Tippy beamed at her. "It's nice to work at something you find rewarding. I didn't realize you did grooming! I'll have to introduce my little Weesa to you."

Myrtle managed with some difficulty not to make a face. Weesa was a tiny scrap of a dog who Tippy had lately been keeping in her purse when she ran errands. She wasn't sure what saved her from having to spend the afternoon with Weesa, but she was thankful for it. Tippy doted on the little dog, but she showed her teeth to Myrtle whenever she saw her. And made most alarming growling sounds.

Worried that Weesa would somehow remotely hijack the conversation, Myrtle quickly said, "Had you seen your father recently, dear?"

Julia shook her head. There was a cool expression on her face. It seemed to Myrtle that perhaps Julia was more concerned about being a suspect in the murder than her father's demise.

"No, I'm afraid not. We'd become somewhat estranged, unfortunately. We hadn't had any contact with each other for a while."

"I see," said Myrtle.

Julia sighed. "All I've ever wanted to do since I was a kid was work with my father. I grew up in those vineyards, running through them, lying on the ground and looking up at the clouds. I couldn't even imagine a time when I wasn't spending every waking hour there."

Myrtle said, "But your father wasn't onboard with your plans to stay there?"

Julia made a face. "Dad always seemed like he was on a mission to upend me. First, he divorced my mom."

Tippy gave her a sympathetic smile. "That must have been a terrible shock."

"It was very immature and unsettling. I felt like my life had been turned upside-down. Then I had the choice of whether to be with my mom or my dad. Mom and I have always gotten along really well, so ordinarily I'd have been with her."

"You and your father weren't as close?" asked Myrtle.

"No. He was always very distant with me. Even when I was a kid, he just wasn't a very warm person to be around. I'd be telling him a story about fairies in the vineyard, and he'd give me a cold look and say I needed to grow up. When I was five."

Myrtle's lips tightened. She liked Gerald less and less. However, that didn't mean he deserved to be poisoned with strychnine, which was a most unpleasant end.

Julia continued, "Even though I'd rather have stayed with Mom, I wanted to be at the vineyard more. I didn't expect Dad to welcome me with open arms, but I didn't expect him to resent me, either."

Now Tippy seemed annoyed by Gerald, too. "Resent you? Whatever for? You were a child."

"Maybe it was because he was dating. I guess maybe he wanted his privacy or to pretend that he didn't have children or responsibilities at all. I made myself as invisible as possible, which was easy enough when I spent most of my time outside." She took a deep breath. "But the worst blow came when I asked Dad to let me work at the vineyard. I'd expected that one day the winery would be mine. I was Dad's only child, after all. But he rebuffed me when I asked to work. He said I was too immature and inexperienced to handle it."

Myrtle frowned. "How did he expect you to gain experience if he didn't allow you to work there? Surely you could have at least pulled weeds or something."

Julia said in a bitter voice, "It didn't make any sense. I realized then he had no intention of letting me be part of the winery. Once I realized that, I moved out right away. And that pretty much fractured our relationship, right then. Which is something the police seem well aware of. That's why I think they're considering me a suspect."

Myrtle said, "Your father could obviously be a difficult man."

Julia gave a short laugh. "That's a nice way of putting it."

"So there must be other people who would make suitable suspects for the police. Can you think of any?"

As much as Tippy disparaged gossip, she seemed very intent on Julia's answer.

"Well, the first person who comes to mind is Frank Hayes," said Julia thoughtfully.

Myrtle said, "Your father's neighbor."

"You know him?" asked Julia, surprised.

"He's done some plumbing work for me in the past. But I also know his mother, Eunice. I understand she's over at Greener Pastures now." Myrtle's expression clearly indicated what she thought of the Greener Pastures decision.

"That's right. Frank's not a bad guy. I've met him a couple of times."

Myrtle said, "I'm surprised that you'd have come in contact with him since you moved out."

Julia said wryly, "Frank made the mistake of thinking I was a decision-maker over at Greystone Grapes. I told him that was the furthest thing from the truth. He'd found my address online and come over to see me."

Tippy said, "I'm a little lost. Why would Frank Hayes have wanted to visit with you? What did he want?"

"Oh, my dad was being a jerk about expanding the vineyard. He'd pressured Frank's mom into selling part of her property. Frank was furious. He was hoping I could convince my dad to sell it back to them."

Myrtle said slowly, "Did Gerald give Frank's mother a fair price for the property?"

"Of course not! It was Dad. He manipulated her. She'd turned him down several times, but Dad kept on pressuring her. When he finally persuaded her to sell the property to him, it was far below its value. He'd made sure he'd gotten himself a real deal." That bitterness was back in Julia's voice again.

Tippy said, "I'm sure Frank *was* furious. He's always seemed very close to his mother and quite protective of her."

Julia nodded. "Exactly. Frank felt like the stress and pressure that Dad piled on his mom to make her sell the land caused his mother's decline. Her land had been in the family for generations and meant everything to her. Now she's so fragile that she needed to go to a retirement home."

Myrtle said, "That certainly sounds like a powerful motive. Was there someone else you could think of, dear?"

Julia gave a small smile. "Isabella also had a motive. I really like her, so I hate to say it. But Dad was pretty awful to her. He totally froze Isabella out the same way he froze me out. She was trying to get information from him and advice on running a vineyard. But he considered her to be competition and wouldn't give her any kind of help. Kind of maddening. But I'm not sure if that's enough of a motive to murder somebody."

Julia looked at her watch. "I should get going. Thanks for letting me talk everything out."

"Was that helpful?" Tippy sounded doubtful, as if the conversation, led mainly by Myrtle, might have traumatized Julia even further.

"Definitely," she said, rising from the prissy armchair. "It's been a tough day today, but now at least I feel like I'm getting a handle on what happened to Dad. Plus, I've made arrangements for the service. Things are moving along."

Myrtle and Tippy followed Julia out to the parking lot. Tippy was asking about the service, and what her various committees could do to help with the reception following. Myrtle was thinking about what Julia had told them. She would have to have that talk with Isabella soon. Even though she was Elaine's friend and seemed like a pleasant young woman, her dealings with Gerald might have led her to murder.

Myrtle climbed back into Tippy's car. She was feeling a bit tired, mostly from spending so much time with Tippy. With Tippy, one always had to be on one's guard to avoid being signed up for volunteering with a mind-boggling array of organizations. Plus, Tippy's perfection was downright draining.

Tippy said, "I'm imagining you need to get home and put your feet up for a little while."

"Yes," said Myrtle, trying to sound feeble. If she sounded feeble, perhaps Tippy wouldn't single her out for more volunteering.

"I haven't forgotten about the store, though," said Tippy. "You just stay in the car, and I'll dash out with supper."

Myrtle was a bit more chipper at the idea of having a ready-made salmon meal from the Piggly Wiggly. She was even more chipper at the idea of not having to pay for it.

Tippy, good as her word, was quickly back in the vehicle with the meal in hand. "Now, it's all ready to eat," she said. "Just pop it in the microwave. You don't even have to turn your oven on."

Myrtle bristled a little. "I might want to warm it in the oven."

Tippy seemed to think that Myrtle might not be able to handle her oven. "You might. But I can attest to the fact that it's just fine in the microwave." She went on to talk lightly about other things while Myrtle scowled and wondered why Tippy believed Myrtle and her oven were incompatible.

"Here we are," said Tippy cheerfully as she pulled into Myrtle's driveway. "Thanks for helping with the clothes closet."

Myrtle managed not to be snippy. "I was happy to help out. Thanks for the salmon."

Tippy beamed at her. "Remember to just use the microwave!"

Myrtle was fully out of the car when she saw Erma peering at them from her front yard. "No," said Myrtle under her breath.

Fortunately, Erma seemed to have Tippy in her sights. "Tippy! Oh, Tippy!"

If Myrtle didn't know better, she'd have thought Tippy said something rather unladylike under her breath. Tippy had her window down, perhaps to offer Myrtle more helpful advice regarding the salmon and microwaving in general. Myrtle smiled grimly as Tippy fell prey to Erma.

"I wanted to tell you all about my yard project," said Erma to Tippy as Myrtle sneaked past her with her bags of books and food.

"Did you?" asked Tippy, sounding rather hopeless at being trapped.

"Yes, indeedy! I tried to call you twice, but you didn't answer."

"Didn't I?" asked Tippy. "Gracious. I'm sorry, Erma. I've been volunteering so much lately. I must not have had my ringer on."

As Tippy fell further into Erma's clutches, Myrtle happily hurried inside, locking the door behind her. Tippy deserved every bit of the next fifteen minutes with Erma. She had the feeling Red had been spreading misinformation about her cooking abilities again. He was getting a kick of telling wretchedly untrue stories about her various cooking failures. But, when one cooked over the course of a lifetime, there were sure to be the occasional minor mishaps.

She worked on her crossword puzzle, then read her new book. It turned out to be a page-turner, and she found herself sitting in her chair, lost in the story. When she next looked up, at the end of the book, it was ten o'clock at night.

"Heavens!" She got out of her chair and turned on the oven, feeling like a revolutionary for doing so. Then she heated her teriyaki salmon. Tippy was right about one thing, at least, thought Myrtle grudgingly. It was delicious.

By the time she'd warmed her meal and eaten it, it was eleven. Myrtle promptly turned in, although her mind was churning with various aspects of Gerald's murder. She fell into an uneasy sleep, which she awakened from at three. Myrtle slid out of bed. She knew better than trying to fall back to sleep when she was as alert as she was.

She pulled on her old bathrobe and her sturdiest slippers and headed right outside. The moon was either nearly full or had just been full and was helpfully lending its light to the sidewalk. Soon she was at Miles's house. Miles was also an insomniac, although he didn't seem to ascribe to the practice as routinely as Myrtle did. She thought she saw a light on in the back of Miles's house. It was enough of a sign for her to ring the doorbell.

It took a minute for Miles to come to the door. When he did, he was wearing his bathrobe over his pajamas. He squinted at her through the side window before quickly opening the door.

"Were you asleep?" asked Myrtle in an accusatory voice.

"Soundly." Miles gave her a baleful look.

"That surprises me. Usually you're awake around now."

Miles could tell when it was time to just give in. "Well, I'm awake now. Want some coffee?"

"Yes. Oh, and do you have any cheese and bread?"

Miles said, "I should be able to dig that up in the kitchen."

"Good. I've had this craving for cheese toast, but I'm out of both items." Myrtle blamed this on Tippy. If Tippy hadn't kidnapped her and forced her to volunteer, she'd have had the time and energy to go to the store and fill up a cart.

Myrtle started a pot of coffee for them while Miles heated the oven and made the cheese toast. Myrtle talked about inconsequential things during the interim, the type of things you might say when you were conversing with someone who'd just woken up and hadn't yet had caffeine. She wanted Miles to be fully awake when she started talking about various suspects, her plans for the day, and the murder.

After twenty minutes, Miles seemed sufficiently awake. Myrtle dove right in. "There have been some developments."

"Developments?"

"That's right. I happened to run into Ben Foster at the library," said Myrtle.

Miles frowned. "That seems rather coincidental. You weren't following him, were you?"

"Of course not! You know the library is a frequent haunt of mine. He was at the library because the police were combing over the vineyard and he couldn't be there. Apparently, he has a cottage on the premises. He seemed like a very nice young man. Unless he's a murderer, of course."

"Of course," said Miles. "Did you give him the third degree?"

"Certainly not. We had a very genial conversation. Ben was eager for information since the police weren't handing much of it out. I filled him in on our discovery of Gerald."

"*Your* discovery of Gerald," said Miles. "I was asleep by the fireplace." He turned slightly pink at the thought of napping in public.

"Anyway, he was most interested. Our conversation continued from there. He had no alibi because he was working on paperwork or some such. And apparently, he did sometimes disagree with Gerald."

Miles raised his eyebrows. "That seems dangerous. Having arguments with your boss."

"I'm not sure he phrased it as having arguments. I believe it was more of a difference of opinion. At any rate, Ben disagreed with the direction Gerald was heading in with the vineyard. He felt the focus was moving away from quality wines and into more of a mass-production, commercial route."

Miles said, "That was enough to murder Gerald?"

"Well, there was some other stuff about pesticides and so forth. You know how folks get very passionate about the environment." Myrtle paused. "Actually, Ben seemed quite passionate about his job, period. So I might see something getting out of hand."

"Did he offer any ideas about who might be responsible for Gerald's death?"

Myrtle said, "Although he really liked Isabella, he thought she could possibly have done it. Gerald hadn't been very helpful when she asked him for help when setting up the winery."

"Surely she didn't expect him to chip in and help her out. After all, she's a competitor."

Myrtle said, "I got the impression she wasn't asking for that much involvement. Just tips. Anyway, Gerald didn't provide them. And he could also apparently be quite rude. But Isabella wasn't the primary person who Ben thought might have killed Gerald. That was Liv Anderson."

"Who's that?" Miles took another sip of his coffee in an attempt to keep up.

"She was Gerald's girlfriend. Ben didn't like her because she always managed to put Gerald in a terrible mood. And Gerald wasn't the kind of person who could keep bad moods to himself."

Miles frowned again. He said slowly, "Why would he continue dating someone who put him in a bad mood?"

"Who knows? People are strange. Ben said Liv was always suspicious that Gerald was having an affair. But Ben didn't think he was. So Liv might just be a paranoid sort of person."

Miles got up to pour himself another cup of coffee. "This is a lot of information to take in."

"Isn't it? And I haven't even gotten to the part where I spoke to Julia."

Miles sat back down again. "Julia?"

"Gerald's estranged daughter."

"You talked to *her*?" asked Miles.

Myrtle said, "You know I usually like having my trusty side-kick with me. But suspects were leaping out of the woodwork yesterday. I had to handle it on my own."

"Julia came out of the woodwork?" asked Miles doubtfully.

"Yes. Out of the woodwork at church."

"*Church?*"

Myrtle scowled at Miles, then said piously, "Yes, Miles, church. I do attend church, you know."

"On the rarest of occasions." He narrowed his eyes. "You're saying that you randomly attended a Sunday morning service yesterday?"

"I'm not saying anything of the kind. I was kidnapped by Tippy yesterday afternoon after seeing Ben Foster at the library. She dragged me over to the church to volunteer by sorting clothes."

Miles took another sip of his coffee and looked even more dubious. "Tippy dragged you to the church."

"Drove me. But it was against my will. I wanted to go back home with my books. But Tippy said the clothing closet was in dire shape and needed sorting. This is all beside the point. Julia Greystone was there to plan her father's memorial service, which will be today. You'll come with me, of course."

Miles shifted uncomfortably. "I never even met the man."

"It's not as if there will be a pop quiz for entry to the service, Miles. And I'm fairly sure you've attended other funerals when you didn't know the deceased."

Miles hesitated. "Probably. But now I'm having second thoughts. Doesn't it seem slightly disrespectful?"

"Not remotely. And it sounds like it will be a lovely service." Myrtle had no idea whether it would be lovely or not, but it would be easier to get Miles to a nice memorial.

Miles said reluctantly, "I suppose so." He paused. "What did you find out from Julia?"

"Well, I think she's had a hard time of it. She grew up on the grounds of that vineyard and adores the place. Julia said she couldn't imagine when she was little that she'd ever be parted from it."

Miles discreetly wiped a couple of cheese toast crumbs from his chin. "Gerald was at fault there, I suppose?"

"That's what Julia claims. She said her father was very condescending toward her when she asked about helping at the vineyard. She was quite hurt, moved away, and has had limited contact with her father since."

Miles said, "But she didn't move to be with her mother."

"No. She said she was closer to her mom, but didn't want to leave the vineyard when she was a child. I suppose that, when she left home more recently, she was too accustomed to life in Bradley to suddenly emigrate to Canada."

Miles thought about this. "I guess Gerald's ex-wife won't be coming to the memorial service, even to support Julia?"

"It's a pretty rushed affair. I'd think it would be stressful to drop everything, pack up one's funeral clothes, and fly to another country at the drop of a hat."

Miles said, "Speaking of funeral clothing, have you spot-checked your funeral outfit?"

Myrtle's funeral garments went through unbelievable transformations in her closet. She'd attend a service, eat carefully and mindfully at the reception, remove the outfit at home, and hang it up. Then, somehow, when she next pulled it out, it would be spattered with something monstrous from the buffet line.

"No, not yet. I'll have to remember to check it," said Myrtle. Then she promptly forgot as she started thinking about Julia again. "I felt rather sorry for Julia. Her mother lives far away, she was estranged from her father, and now she's embroiled in a murder."

"And the service is today," said Miles. "Which seems very speedy."

"Yes. I think she's wanting to move forward and put it all behind her. I wonder what Gerald's will is going to mean for Julia."

Miles said, "Surely Gerald would leave the vineyard to Julia. Who else is there?"

Myrtle shrugged. "Maybe Gerald didn't even leave a will behind. Sometimes those bigger-than-life types can assume they'll live forever. In that case, the property will have to go through probate court."

"I can't imagine a father doing that to his daughter," said Miles in a disapproving tone.

"That's because you were an excellent father. He *might* have left a will behind. Maybe he did the right thing. Or maybe he left the whole vineyard to charity. Who knows?"

Miles said, "Did Julia say who else might be a suspect?"

"Well, she mentioned Frank Hayes."

"Ah," said Miles. "The man we met when we were leaving the winery."

"That's right. According to Julia, her father had pressured Frank's mother into selling the property for an unfair price."

Miles made a face. "I'm sure that upset Frank."

"Exactly. And then he had to suddenly become Gerald's neighbor after Frank's mom ends up in Greener Pastures. It doesn't sound as if they were friendly. Julia said that Frank blamed Gerald for his mother's health decline. The property had been in her family for generations and she loved the place."

Miles said, "That sounds like the kind of stress that could affect someone's health." He paused. "I'm liking Gerald less and less."

"I don't think he was the easiest person to deal with. Which might be why he ended up poisoned."

Miles shifted uneasily at the thought of poison. "Although Gerald seemed like a rather despicable person, I don't think he deserved to die in such a horrible way. Strychnine, you said?"

"Strychnine," said Myrtle. "At least he exhibited all the signs. He was quite contorted."

Miles carefully put down his cheese toast. "I don't want to think about that. Let's move on to brighter subjects."

Myrtle tried to think of one. Her mind kept returning to murder, no matter how hard she attempted to steer it in other directions. Finally, she said, "We could watch TV."

"Yes," said Miles in relief. "Let's do that."

Of course, at that early hour of the morning, the options were rather limited. There was a fishing show on featuring a man carefully explaining the type of bait and the lure he was using to hook fish. Another option was a sitcom with a particularly tiresome laugh track. Naturally, there was an infomercial on beauty and skincare secrets. The news was on, as it always was, but it was hardly a relaxing option for two seniors up in the wee hours of the morning.

With relief, Miles found a nature documentary. "Here we go. This should be a safe option."

Myrtle said, "What's the topic? I hope it's penguins. I've been in the mood to see penguins lately. Or that other cold weather bird."

"Terns?"

"No, not that one," said Myrtle.

"The snowy owl?"

Myrtle looked at him. "Miles, I suspect you've been watching entirely too many nature shows. No, I mean a bird that people know about. A bird that's very cute."

"Ah. Puffins."

"That's the one," said Myrtle, beaming at him. "Is that what's playing now?"

Miles pulled up the guide on the TV. "Hmm. No. It says here it's a show called 'Glowing Caves: Subterranean Luminescence.'"

"Oh boy," said Myrtle.

"The description sounds pretty interesting. *Descend into underground caves to witness the otherworldly beauty of organisms that emit light in the depths of darkness, creating a natural light show beneath the Earth's surface.*"

Myrtle wasn't completely convinced.

"It has to be better than the infomercial on expensive skin exfoliants," said Miles reasonably.

And so they settled on the cave show. Miles was able to put thoughts of poison behind him enough to make and consume more cheese toast. And the two friends spent the early morning hours in companionable quiet.

Chapter Eight

Hours later, Myrtle was back home and getting ready for Gerald's memorial service. She'd persuaded the reluctant Miles to not only attend, but to pick her up. To her dismay, she realized she'd forgotten to check the condition of her funeral outfit when she'd returned home. To be fair, Pasha had shown up ravenous, and Myrtle had been focused on finding something yummy for her favorite carnivore. After that, the newspaper arrived, and she'd been absorbed in trying to figure out a particular clue for the crossword. *Enigmatic tome hides vexing question*. Eight letters. Then she rolled her eyes and carefully wrote *mysterious* in the blanks. The lack of sleep last night was starting to show.

That's why she hadn't remembered to check her outfit. And now it was time to get dressed and her outfit had all sorts of greasy stains on it. Myrtle scowled at the garment. There was nothing to do but mix-and-match something else. She was able to find a pair of black slacks. The problem was to locate a top that wasn't altogether too cheerful for Gerald's service. If Myrtle looked at all cheerful or bright, she was certain Miles wouldn't want to attend the memorial whatsoever. He was already on the fence about it enough as it was.

But her closet seemed full of chirpy colors. She rummaged further into the back and found a horrid brown blouse that she'd clearly deliberately shoved as far away as possible. It would have to do. She pulled out the iron and touched it up. Then she realized she'd burned the blouse with the iron near the hem. Myrtle gritted her teeth. She'd have to tuck in the blouse. But that meant she'd have to find a belt for the pants. Finally, she found a belt that wasn't too garish. Apparently, most of her belt collection had been established in the 1980s.

She was finished just in time. Miles tapped lightly at her door. Myrtle pulled a brush through her wayward hair and then hurried to the door.

"New outfit?" asked Miles slowly. "I don't think I've seen you wear that before."

"It's a hidden gem," said Myrtle in a terse voice. "Let's head on out. There might be quite a few people at the service."

"People who were fond of Gerald?" asked Miles as they walked outside.

"People who like wine. I'm sure they're wondering if Julia is going to let everyone sample the goods."

Miles said, "Do you think she will?"

"Doubtful. It's not a wake, after all. And Julia didn't even seem fond of her dad. Besides, if the reception is held in the church dining hall, there will be no alcohol allowed."

When they arrived, Myrtle saw the sanctuary was decorated as she expected—sparingly. There was a single lit candle at the front of the church on the memorial table. She saw a few sparse flower arrangements.

The organist was playing a soft instrumental hymn as everyone came in, greeted one another, and quietly took their seats.

Right before the service started, Julia came in with an elderly woman. They sat in the front pew.

"That's Julia," said Myrtle.

"Is she with Gerald's mother?" asked Miles.

"Both his parents are long-dead. That must be Julia's maternal grandmother."

Myrtle's prediction about the number of attendees was true. There was standing room only by the time the service started. Myrtle saw Red glowering across the sanctuary at her from the back row. She blew him a kiss.

Also in attendance were Ben Foster, who seemed to look in Julia's direction instead of at the front of the church; Frank Hayes, who looked mildly irritated; and Isabella, who had a hard time staying still.

"Does it seem strange that Frank Hayes is here?" asked Miles.

"He's probably trying to prove to Red that he had no hard feelings against Gerald."

"Is Red here?" asked Miles, craning his neck.

"Sadly, yes. I wish Lieutenant Perkins was here instead. But I've already spotted Red giving me a menacing look from across the sanctuary."

The service was short and sweet. There were two hymns, sung by a soloist. There was a Bible reading. And there was a homily given by the minister. No eulogies by Julia or anyone else.

Then it was off to the church hall for the reception. Miles said, "We could just head back home."

"Nonsense! I'd like to speak with Liv Anderson, Gerald's girlfriend."

"How will you manage to do that?" asked Miles. "You don't even know the woman."

"I looked her up online. I'll be able to recognize her easily. And don't worry. I'll be able to wrangle a conversation with Liv with no problems at all. I'm very good at manipulating people."

"I'm well aware," said Miles dryly, obviously feeling quite manipulated by the fact he was even at the service.

"I'll simply be welcoming. Greet her by name. Be sympathetic. And I'll be a fantastic listener. She'll gravitate right over to me," said Myrtle.

However, things didn't go quite that easily. After Myrtle and Miles had gone through the buffet line with the church ladies spooning out gobs of Southern casseroles, fried vegetables, and various biscuit combinations on their plates, Liv seemed to be still standing in the doorway, trying to figure out what she should do. She was in her 40s with brown hair and a stylish dress.

"Maybe she thinks people have to pay for the food. She might not realize it's brought in by volunteers," said Miles.

"I'm going to invite her to sit with us."

Miles sighed. He knew by now when there was no chance of dissuading Myrtle.

Myrtle carefully affected old lady fragility again, leaning on her cane so that her height was hidden as well as possible. She beamed at Liv, who looked rather confused.

"Well goodness! Liv Anderson. It's good to see you. It's been a long time, hasn't it?"

This approach thoroughly knocked Liv off-balance. She clearly had no idea who Myrtle was. This was fair, since Myrtle had never met her. But Liv had obviously been raised right. You didn't argue with old ladies. You didn't question them. And you certainly didn't tell them you don't remember who they are.

"Hi there," said Liv brightly. "Yes, it's been a while."

Myrtle then gave her a mournful look. "I've been thinking about you. What a terrible thing, losing Gerald like that. So very sudden. You must be struggling to even take it all in."

Liv, fortunately, seemed to want to talk about her troubles. "I have been, yes, even though I've been awake every night trying to sort it out in my head."

"You poor thing," crooned Myrtle. "I'm so very sorry." She gestured over to the table where Miles sat, looking uncomfortable. "You'll have to join my friend Miles and me at our table. Tell me all about it. Maybe it will help you feel better."

"Okay," said Liv slowly. She glanced over at the buffet again. "Should I . . . I mean, is there a place to pay?"

Miles had been right. Myrtle said, "Oh, it's complimentary. Donated by church committee members. And it's always delicious food. Get a plate and join us."

"Okay," said Liv, looking a bit more cheerful at having some direction.

Myrtle joined Miles again. "Mission accomplished?" he asked dryly.

"Of course. It was a piece of cake." Myrtle paused. "She thought she had to pay for the food."

Miles swallowed down a bit of fried okra. "I figured she might."

"I don't understand how someone can be in their forties and not be familiar with funeral protocol."

Miles said, "Perhaps she's been lucky and hasn't lost anyone until now. Forty isn't that old."

"To *us*. Age is relative."

Miles pushed some of the food around on his plate. Myrtle frowned at him. "You're not eating much."

"It's very heavy, isn't it? Sort of like the food at the diner."

Myrtle said, "It's traditional Southern cooking. It won't be light. Just take your blood pressure medicine when you get back home and you should be just fine."

Miles nibbled at some green bean casserole. "Even the vegetables are as unhealthy as possible."

"Of course they are! Southern food, remember? But everything tastes good."

Even Miles couldn't argue with that.

Soon Liv joined them. She didn't seem to share Miles's anxiety about heavy Southern dishes, considering the way her plate was loaded down with them. She gave them a rueful glance. "I got carried away."

"As you should," said Myrtle. "You were faced with too many options." She quickly introduced Miles, and they chatted for a couple of minutes on inconsequential things while Liv got her bearings.

Then Myrtle dove on in. But instead of jumping in with questions regarding the murder, she decided to get Liv warmed up a little first. "Liv, the service was lovely. I'm guessing you and Julia planned it?"

She could tell by Liv's expression that this was absolutely the right way to have hooked Liv. She immediately made a face. "Julia wouldn't let me have a thing to do with it. It was a nice enough service, but I'd have made sure there was some pizazz."

Myrtle was sure she would have. That, perhaps, was why Julia hadn't wanted her to be involved.

"I told Julia that she and her father weren't close enough for Julia to know the kind of service Gerald would have wanted. But she wouldn't listen to me. In fact, she was furious. That's when she told me she was planning Gerald's memorial service completely by herself." Liv stopped speaking, fuming to herself at the memory.

"Mercy," said Myrtle. "That seems like something of an overreaction, doesn't it? What type of service would Gerald have wanted?"

"Oh, you know Gerald. He was a showman. He had these events at the winery—he'd bring in bands, caterers. He liked the big shindigs. Gerald liked it when people talked. This service," said Liv with a sniff, "is going to be quickly forgotten. He'd have wanted it over at the vineyard."

"The memorial service?" asked Miles. His voice was unintentionally scandalized at a service being held in a vineyard. He blushed a little.

Liv smiled at him, and Miles blushed a bit more. "No, I think he'd have wanted a church service. But the *reception* would have been at the vineyard. Can you think of a better place?"

Since Liv appeared to be waiting for an answer, Miles hastily shook his head.

Myrtle noticed Julia was walking around the church hall, making sure everyone had food and knew where the drinks table was. Everything was running smoothly, and Myrtle couldn't help but think that Julia would have done an excellent job at running the vineyard and winery.

Liv followed Myrtle's gaze and snorted. "Now everything is just as Julia wanted. She'll be back at the vineyard."

Myrtle said in a low, gossipy voice, "Do you think Julia had something to do with Gerald's death?"

Liv shrugged. "I have no idea what goes through Julia's head."

"I do understand that Julia and her father had been estranged and hadn't spoken in some time."

"Not true," said Liv immediately. "The two of them had a huge argument only a week ago. Gerald was grumbling about it right up until his death on Saturday."

This was certainly news. Julia had said they hadn't been in touch in a long while. But then, maybe Julia was trying not to be more of a suspect than she already was. "Poor thing," said Myrtle. "Julia must feel terrible about having an argument with her dad right before he died."

Liv seemed eager to talk about Julia. "The problem was that Julia was brought up spoiled and thought she should always get her own way. She thinks way too much of herself."

This was a unique take on Julia. When Myrtle had spoken with Tippy, Tippy had thought entirely the opposite. And, as annoying as Tippy was, Myrtle put a lot of stock in her opinion. Liv, on the other hand, most likely had a case of sour grapes.

Liv was looking across the church hall at Red, eyes narrowed. Red was looking their way too, with *his* eyes narrowed. Liv didn't appear to realize Red was frowning at his mother, not at her. "The police need to open their eyes," she finally said sharply. "Julia's an obvious suspect. Instead, they're wasting their time talking to *me* all the time. I wasn't anywhere close to Serenity Springs. Gerald had asked me to go with him, but I wasn't in the mood to hang out with people. I was just hanging out at the house." She paused. "I might have been a little hungover from the night before. Gerald and I entertained on Friday night and things went a bit longer than I'd planned on."

Myrtle said, "Why was Gerald so interested in going over to Serenity Springs? Was it a case of wanting to check out the competition?"

"As if!" said Liv with another snort. "Gerald knew Greystone Grapes wine would be far superior in every way."

"Was he going to give Isabella advice? I'd think Isabella would be dying to get help from an expert like Gerald."

Liv shook her head emphatically, brown hair swaying from side to side. "Nope. He was just going to sit back and watch her fail. He planned on critiquing the wines for a publication, and he wasn't going to be complimentary. You know he was a wine critic?"

Myrtle and Miles nodded.

"I'm sure the publicity wouldn't have been good for Isabella," said Liv with a shrug. "But that's how you learn and get better, right? It was almost like Gerald was doing her a favor."

Myrtle had the feeling that Isabella wouldn't have thought of it quite that way.

Liv's expression was brooding as she watched Julia speak with Isabella across the room. "The other person who wanted to do in Gerald was Julia."

Chapter Nine

"Mercy," said Myrtle. "Are you sure?"

A flicker of annoyance crossed Liv's features. "Of course I am. Everyone seems to think Julia is this sweet girl who does nothing wrong. Nothing could be further from the truth." Her mouth tightened. "Do you know, she gave me a deadline for moving off the vineyard property? Julia said she'd call the cops on me and tell them I'm trespassing."

Myrtle said, "Is the deadline generous?"

"There's *nothing* generous about it. But I think Julia's in for an unpleasant surprise. I believe Gerald wrote her out of his will."

"Did he mention he was going to do that?" asked Miles.

Liv shrugged. "He talked about it. Gerald considered Julia a disappointment. I think he'd always wanted a son and couldn't connect with a daughter. He'd already changed his will once, after he divorced Julia's mother. It makes sense that he'd be open to keeping it updated. Besides, Gerald mentioned he'd like to provide for me in his will. We'd been seeing each other for a while, you know. Anyway, I think the unveiling of the will could be an unpleasant event for Julia." She leaned in closer. "Maybe she got wind of the fact that her father was going to change the will. They'd argued just recently and that might have been something that Gerald let slip in the heat of the moment. I'd say *that's* a motive."

Liv's gaze moved across the room again, this time lighting on Red once more. "I can't believe the cops think I had something to do with this. Gerald and I were perfectly happy with each other. Two peas in a pod."

Myrtle asked, "How did the two of you meet?"

Liv's mouth curled up in a reminiscent smile. "A couple of my girlfriends wanted to go out for drinks. They were determined to choose some scruffy bar downtown, but I persuaded them to go more upscale. Besides, Gerald had a band out there that day, so we'd get free entertainment at the same time. So there we were, hanging out, laughing it up with our wine. Gerald was there, behind the bar."

"Working the bar?" asked Myrtle. "Somehow I thought he'd stopped doing most of the work at the winery."

"Oh, he wasn't working. He was talking to the bartender. Maybe making sure they were on the same page or something. Anyway, he kept looking over at our group, smiling at me. I smiled back." She shrugged. "The rest is history."

"Did the two of you have much in common?" Myrtle asked. She thought about the age difference between them, and the fact that Ben Foster had reported lots of arguments between Gerald and Liv.

"Oh sure, we had plenty in common. Both of us liked funny movies. And having a good time. Gerald had reached the age where he could just sort of oversee the operations at the winery and take time off. We were both interested in traveling." Her expression darkened. "We didn't get a chance to do it, though. Which really makes me mad."

Her focus returned to Julia, and she grimaced. "Julia's heading this direction. That's my cue to get out of here." She stood up. "Good seeing you." And she was quickly gone.

Miles said uneasily, "Maybe we should go, too. I don't fancy having to tell Julia what my fictitious connection with her father was."

"Nonsense. You don't have to say a word. You can sit here, look sympathetic, and be the strong, silent type."

Miles seemed to have doubts about whether he could pull that off.

"Besides, I want to speak with Julia again. Ben Foster appears to be head over heels with her."

Now Miles was even more alarmed than he'd been previously. "You're not going to do any matchmaking, are you? Not here at her father's memorial service."

"For heaven's sake, Miles, I'm simply going to put a bug in her ear. I'm not going to drag her and Ben to the altar. I thought she might be interested in having something good happen, amid all this mess."

Miles was unconvinced. "Julia may not be remotely interested in Ben Foster."

"But what if she is? Wouldn't she rather know?"

Miles gave her a stern look. Myrtle huffed out a sigh. "All right, all right. You're giving me Red Clover looks. I'll focus on Ben, then. He's here at the reception."

Their debate was cut short by Julia's appearance at their table. She smiled at them. "It's so good of you both to come out."

Myrtle said, "Of course we're here. We wouldn't be anywhere else."

Miles gave Julia a nervous smile. "I'm Miles Bradford."

"Thanks for being here, Mr. Bradford." She turned to Myrtle. "No news on the investigation, I'm guessing?"

Myrtle shook her head. "Red operates like a vault when it comes to investigations." It occurred to her, though, that she hadn't had the chance to speak with her favorite member of the state police, Lieutenant Perkins. She'd have to call him. Occasionally, he'd be kind enough to give her a snippet of helpful information. At least he was more useful than Red with such matters.

Julia looked disappointed, but nodded. "He seems like he'd be very professional." She glanced around the room. "It was good seeing you."

As she moved away, Miles let out a pent-up breath. "Now we've spoken with Julia. Ready to head back home?"

But Myrtle was eyeing Ben Foster.

Miles sighed. "You've got Ben Foster in your sights."

"Well, it does make sense to start the matchmaking process when both parties are at the same place."

Miles said, "Both of the parties or both of the victims?"

"Don't be obstreperous, Miles! I'm just helping a potential relationship along. I live in Bradley, North Carolina and don't have a lot to do. Humor me."

"Go right ahead. I'll wait at the table for you and finish up my glass of sweet tea."

So Myrtle headed across the room to where Ben Foster was sitting, alone, at one table. He was so entirely focused on Julia that he didn't see Myrtle approach him.

He stood up when he did. "Miss Myrtle! Nice to see you."

She smiled at him and waved him to sit down again, where she joined him. "Hi there, Ben. I won't be but a minute because my ride is ready to head back home. But I wanted to let you know I was speaking with Julia and she told me how much she respects you."

Ben immediately turned pink and flustered. "Did she?" His voice squeaked.

Myrtle nodded. "Yes. And she thinks you're so very accomplished and interesting."

Ben's gaze followed Julia again. "But what should I do? This seems like a terrible time to ask her out. Wouldn't it be very presumptuous? She's struggling with her father's death and everything else that goes along with it."

Myrtle wasn't at all sure that Julia was struggling at all. If anything, she seemed energized and focused. But then, she'd been wanting to be back at the vineyard for ages, and her father had been her only real obstacle. "I think asking her out right now would make a delightful distraction for Julia."

Ben still wavered. "I don't know."

"Maybe just ask her out for a coffee? Or a drink. Those are pretty easy dates, and short ones."

Ben nodded, looking across the room again. "Okay. Maybe I'll just stick around and see if Julia wants a coffee after the service. It's early for a drink."

"Good idea," said Myrtle. "Good luck to you." And with that, she headed back over to Miles.

Soon, they were both in his car and driving back.

"What are your plans for this afternoon?" asked Myrtle.

Miles said, "I'm completely exhausted. That service really took it out of me."

"How on earth is that even possible? It was the most innocuous of services. We've gone to far more elaborate ones. Ones with choirs and chamber orchestras and eulogies that went on for an hour."

"Don't remind me," said Miles. "Anyway, I'm going to put my feet up for a while. After all, we didn't get much sleep last night." The last words were put rather pointedly.

Myrtle, however, was thinking of other things. "At least we had the chance to speak with Liv at the reception. What was your impression of her?"

"Well, she didn't seem like the harridan Ben had told you she was. And didn't Julia give you a poor impression of her, too?"

Myrtle said, "She did. I'm more inclined to listen to Ben, since he's not family. He'd said Liv brought out the worst in Gerald, and then Gerald passed along his bad mood to everyone else."

"She was certainly on her best behavior at the reception," said Miles.

"Yes. But she would be, wouldn't she? The police were there. Plus, she was playing the role of the grieving girlfriend."

"Although she didn't seem to be that torn-up over Gerald's demise," said Miles.

"No, but we've seen people grieve in different ways. She seemed more upset about Julia than anything else."

Miles nodded as he pulled into Myrtle's driveway. "True. It sounded like Julia really stepped on Liv's toes with planning the service."

"I was thinking more about the fact Julia gave Liv a deadline to leave. It sounds as if Julia is ready to move right into the vineyard. I can't really blame her, though. After all, she's waited a long time to get back home."

Miles said, "What did you make of what Liv said about the will? Do you think Gerald was planning on changing it?"

"It sounded very much like wishful thinking to me, on Liv's part. Or perhaps an attempt to give Julia a motive for murder. She intimated that Julia was trying to get rid of Gerald before he had the chance to create a new will."

Miles said, "But if that argument was as bad as Liv was saying, it seems like Gerald might have gotten the new will right away."

"I'm still finding it hard to believe that Gerald wouldn't give his daughter the vineyard. It's a *family* business. That's the whole point of it. If he truly was going to give it to a charity to sell or some such, it's just ridiculous." Myrtle shook her head. "Although he was a stubborn man."

Miles suddenly looked alarmed. "Myrtle, Erma is coming outside." They were both still sitting in Miles's car in Myrtle's driveway.

"Oh, for heaven's sake. I'm in no mood to deal with Erma's foolishness today. Maybe she hasn't spotted that we're sitting in the car."

But, naturally, she had. Erma's rat-like face broke into a leering grin, and she waved emphatically at both of them.

Miles said, "Well, bye, Myrtle."

Myrtle glared at him. "You're usually such a gentleman. And now you're rushing me out of your car for the sole purpose of saving yourself from an Erma encounter."

"I sure am," said Miles fervently. "I've reached my quota of things I didn't want to do today. Having one more might push me over the edge."

Myrtle scowled at him. "Fine." She had more to say on the subject, but then realized she needed Miles tomorrow. Or rather, Miles's car. The only problem is that Miles's car usually came with Miles. "Hey, I'm planning on returning to Serenity Springs tomorrow to interview Isabella. You'll come along, won't you?"

Miles looked uneasy, possibly because of the thought of poisoned wine. "We won't be drinking, will we?"

"Of course not. I'll be there on business. You can just sit by the fireplace and fall asleep again, if you want."

Miles colored. "I won't be doing that. I'll just bring my book along. Have you set things up with Isabella?"

"Not yet. I'll call her when I get inside. It shouldn't be an issue. I know she's probably dying for a good write-up in the paper after the disaster on Saturday."

Miles suddenly said in a panic, "Erma's walking this way. Bye, Myrtle."

Myrtle climbed out of Miles's car, and he sped off with a wave to Erma. Myrtle sighed.

"Whatcha doing?" asked Erma as she approached.

"I'm trying to get back inside my house."

Erma gave her braying laugh. "Talk about stating the obvious! Listen, I wanted to see what you thought of my yard so far."

Myrtle spared an unwilling glance over at her neighbor's yard. It was a total disaster. There were little springs of grass trying valiantly to survive. Everything else was just the red clay that passed for soil in their neck of the woods.

"Well, it looks like you did a good job getting rid of all the weeds," said Myrtle.

"Yeah! I didn't realize all that stuff wasn't grass. I mean, it was green, so I figured that's what really counted."

Myrtle wondered once again how all the hours of Erma's garden club attendance could have resulted in this outcome.

"It's a good start," said Myrtle. "I suppose you're going to aerate it now? Then seed and fertilize?"

Erma frowned. "Aerate? Should I do that?"

"It's packed red clay, Erma. You want the ground to be receptive to the seeds." Myrtle stopped herself. This was a problem. She was setting herself up to be Erma's yard expert. This was decidedly not a position she wanted to hold. "You know what? I don't know a lot more than that. Tippy, though, is a genuine expert. Aside from a yard care professional, of course. And a professional is going to charge you for the information. Tippy would just be happy to help." The last bit was said somewhat viciously. Tippy deserved to be thrown under the bus after kidnapping Myrtle.

Erma beamed at her. "Great idea! I'll give her a call."

"Good. See you later, Erma." Although, not if Myrtle saw her first.

Chapter Ten

Myrtle hurried inside, bolting the door behind her. Then she picked up her phone and called Serenity Springs.

Isabella answered right away. From what Myrtle could hear, it was very quiet in the winery. But then, it was a Monday in the early afternoon.

"Isabella? It's Myrtle Clover, Elaine's mother-in-law."

"Mrs. Clover! Nice of you to call."

Myrtle said, "Well, I had something of an ulterior motive. I thought I might come by tomorrow morning so that we could do our talk for the paper."

"That would be perfect, Mrs. Clover. I'll be here. Will you be taking pictures, too?"

Myrtle hadn't really thought about this. But she had a phone that was supposed to take fairly decent photos. "Yes. Pictures will complement the article, won't they? What time should I slide by?"

"Anytime. Like I said, I'll be here."

Myrtle said, "I'll shoot for late-morning. See you then."

The next morning, Myrtle had a big breakfast of grits, eggs, and toast. After a couple of cups of coffee, she worked on her crossword and the sudoku. She was trying to be very careful about calling Miles too early. She'd called him after she'd spoken with Isabella, and they'd made some rough plans. It was nine-thirty, and she was chomping on the bit to get started, regardless of telling Isabella that she'd be there in the late-morning. But Miles had seemed on the verge of cranky yesterday, and she wanted to make sure he'd had enough sleep last night.

Finally, Miles tapped at her door at ten-thirty. Myrtle was pleased to see that he appeared well-rested. He was wearing his customary khaki pants and a button-down shirt.

"Your carriage awaits," he said with a grin.

Myrtle smiled back at him as they walked toward the car. She was relieved to see there was no sign of Erma.

Miles saw the direction of her gaze. "Were you able to rid yourself of Erma fairly quickly yesterday?"

"Not quickly enough. But I was able to eventually foist her on Tippy."

Miles quirked an eyebrow as they got into his car. "What has Tippy done to you?"

"The kidnapping, remember? And the forced labor. I'm totally happy to sort clothing and volunteer, but doing things on Tippy's timetable is annoying."

Miles smiled. "I'm just imagining Tippy as a kidnapper."

"She would actually make an excellent criminal mastermind. She's very organized and thinks everything out. If Tippy were a murderer, we'd have a tough time getting evidence against her. Anyway, she's very aggravating. I didn't want to go over to the church."

Miles started up the car. "On the upside, you were able to talk to Julia there. So perhaps Tippy did you a favor."

"That was totally accidental. At any rate, Tippy is much better with Erma than I am. And she likely knows more about grass." The last was a complete fabrication, but Myrtle was ready to talk about other things.

Miles said, "So the article you're writing on Isabella is going to be a puff-piece, I guess."

"Well, it's certainly not going to be hard-hitting journalism. The idea is to get people over to Serenity Springs, poison or no poison. Elaine seemed very concerned about Isabella."

Miles said, "For good reason. Isabella must have poured a ton of money into the winery. Not only that, but many hours of work. Now it feels as if it's been tainted by this murder."

"Clearly, the murderer was an opportunist. They didn't care if the murder hurt Isabella's business or not."

"How did the murderer know Gerald was going to be over at Isabella's, anyway? It does sound as if he might have just seized the opportunity to kill him," said Miles slowly.

"The only problem with that is the fact they'd have to have been carrying strychnine around on them. That seems rather unlikely."

"Not necessarily," said Miles. "Maybe they'd just been looking for the right opportunity. They could have been carrying a small vial of poison on them for a while."

Myrtle shook her head. "It seems more likely that Gerald talked about his plans to go to Serenity Springs with *someone*. Someone he shouldn't have trusted. Then that person showed up, too, with their baggie of poison."

Miles considered this. "But he apparently wasn't even on speaking terms with his daughter. If it was Julia, how would she know?"

"Maybe she heard it from someone else. Or maybe she was stalking her father and looking for the perfect chance to stick rat poison in his drink."

Miles pulled into the Serenity Springs parking lot. "Another thing I've been wondering is how the killer even got the opportunity to tamper with Gerald's drink."

Myrtle gave him an annoyed look. "You've been wondering about a lot lately."

"It's a sidekick's job," said Miles with dignity.

Myrtle sighed. "All right. Well, I'm assuming that Gerald wasn't exactly watching his drink like a hawk. There were people coming and going around the firepit. Maybe he was even talking up Greystone Grapes at the same time. I can totally see Gerald saying, 'Hey, if you think *this* garbage is any good, you're *really* going to enjoy the wines at my winery.'"

"True," said Miles. "I can imagine him doing that."

"And then the killer, while he's diverted, could have casually tampered with Gerald's drink. I remember he had a glass of red wine in front of him. It could have hidden the bitterness."

"Mm," said Miles. He paused. "But doesn't it seem like a huge risk for the killer? Tampering with a drink that's so close to both Gerald and whomever is the distraction?"

"Perhaps the killer switched drinks with Gerald, put the poison in, and then switched them back."

Miles smiled. "I think there was a Bugs Bunny cartoon that had that same scenario."

"Likely where I pulled it from. Now, are we finally ready to go speak with Isabella? Or are we going to continue sitting in your car while you come up with all sorts of complications?"

"I'm ready," said Miles.

They hopped out of the car. Myrtle had her notebook with her, as well as her phone. She was ready to voice record the interview in case she missed anything. The October leaves were just beginning to fall, and the morning air was crisp. There was something about fall that made a person feel a little more alive.

Myrtle and Miles walked up to the large doors. "I hope there aren't many people here," said Myrtle. "I mean, of course I *want* Isabella to have business, but it would be rather inconvenient for them to be there when I'm trying to interview Isabella."

"The parking lot is empty except for our car and one other. The other one is probably Isabella's."

Myrtle said, "Yes, but more people might come in."

"She was fully staffed on Saturday."

Myrtle said, "That was a big day, though. I'm wondering if maybe she's trying to handle the bartending herself during the week. It's not as busy as the weekend, after all."

When they walked to the door, there was a sign up that the winery would be closed until the upcoming weekend.

"Probably out of respect for Gerald and his family," said Myrtle. "It makes sense.

Inside the winery, it was very quiet. And there seemed to be no sign of Isabella.

"Maybe she's in the back," said Myrtle.

"You got the day right, didn't you? She didn't want *next* week, did she?"

Myrtle gave him an irritated look. "Of course she didn't. It's today. Maybe she's taking a phone call or something."

But it just didn't seem right. The big doors had chimes on them so the staff could hear when a customer arrived. And Isabella was expecting Myrtle, after all. Plus, it was just so very silent there.

Myrtle walked over to the bar. Miles frowned. "You're not going to help yourself to a beverage, are you?" He apparently thought Myrtle was in the frame of mind to break all sorts of rules.

Myrtle glared at him but didn't answer. Instead, she walked to the other side of the large wooden bar. There she found what she was worried she might. Isabella Montague, dead.

Chapter Eleven

"We have a problem," said Myrtle.

Miles had wandered over to the gas fireplace, wanting to put as much distance between himself and Myrtle as possible when Myrtle was nosing around.

"You got the dates wrong?"

"No," said Myrtle briskly. "Isabella is dead. She's been stabbed with what looks like a pruning knife of some kind."

"No."

"Yes, I'm afraid so. I've tried to find a pulse, but there's not one. We'll need to call Red."

Miles took his phone out, fumbling as he tried to find Red in his contacts list. "This is just unbelievable."

"Is it?" asked Myrtle. "It seems like this happens rather a lot to us."

"It does, of course. But, really, we could look like prime suspects. You're the one who found Gerald by the firepit. You're the one who found Isabella, although she was hidden by the bar. We're the only ones here, Myrtle."

Myrtle's eyes narrowed. "Red wouldn't dare consider me a suspect."

"It might be a good way to get rid of you for good. Greener Pastures wouldn't be as effective, considering they don't lock their residents up." Miles found the number and dialed it, taking a deep breath.

Myrtle took the opportunity to look around her. There didn't seem to be anything out of place. The tasting room was just as tidy as it had been on Saturday. The cash register was closed, and there was no evidence of a robbery. Myrtle had the terrible feeling that Isabella had known something about Gerald's death. And the killer had needed to make sure she stayed quiet.

Miles was saying, "Yes, Red, that's right. Yes. No, your mom is fine. She wasn't actually snooping at all; she was here to interview Isabella for *The Bugle*. Sort of a promotional article that was intended to make Serenity Springs look good. What? All right. Yes, we'll wait outside." He turned to tell Myrtle.

"I already heard," she said. "Let's go sit in your car."

When they reached the car, both of them found they were shivering. "Shock," said Miles. "Or maybe a smidge of fear. We might have walked in on the killer, you know. They could still be lurking around here. Maybe they murdered Isabella just moments before we arrived." Miles turned up in the heat in the car.

"I think you and I could have taken them on," said Myrtle. "Maybe it's a pity we didn't come across them." She rubbed at her forehead, which was housing a tiny little headache. "And now we have to deal with Red. It's all very annoying."

Miles said, "But we're having a much better day than Isabella."

Myrtle gave a grim smile. "That's for sure. That poor young woman with her whole life ahead of her. And she'd just started the winery, which had been her dream, according to Elaine. It's a terrible thing."

"We're assuming she knew who Gerald's murderer was."

Myrtle nodded. "She must have. I mean, she didn't *seem* to, when we were talking with her. But maybe something occurred to her later. Or maybe she saw something that seemed like an important clue. After all, she was all over the winery during the tasting. Inside, outside. She was refilling drinks, talking to people, and generally keeping an eye on it all. If anyone was going to see something suspicious, it would have been Isabella."

Miles said, "That's true." He paused. "What's going to happen to the winery, do you think?"

Myrtle sighed. "That's the big question, isn't it? I'd imagine a place like Greystone Grapes would be happy to take over the vineyard here. They could easily expand. Maybe they'd even like having a second tasting room where they could put on indoor music events."

"Isabella wasn't married, was she?" asked Miles.

"No. I believe Elaine has mentioned her having a sister, though. Or maybe the sister joined them for coffee once or twice near the holidays. Something like that. As far as I know, that's Isabella's closest family. I'd imagine whoever is running Greystone Grapes would make her a substantial offer."

Miles said, "Julia, surely. No matter what Liv thought about Gerald changing his will, it's still hard to imagine that he'd cut his daughter out of the family business."

Their musings were interrupted by Red's arrival. He pulled in next to them, glowering at Myrtle. She gave him a wink. The wink didn't appear to improve Red's temper.

"Did you trample all over the evidence?" growled Red as he hopped out of his police cruiser.

"I did my best," said Myrtle, rolling her eyes. "No, Red, of *course* I didn't trample anything. Although there's no *evident* evidence, if you know what I mean. I'd imagine it would be very hard to collect it, anyway. You might find fingerprints, but it's a public business. There were no muddy footprints or anything helpful like that."

"Well, there might be all sorts of fiber or DNA evidence."

"The answer is still no, Red. We didn't trample anything. Miles and I walked in, looked around for Isabella, then I peeped around the side of the bar. I saw Isabella and that she'd been stabbed."

Red asked, "Did you move her at all?"

"Certainly not. I felt for a non-existent pulse, but that was all. I left her *in situ*."

Red didn't appear to appreciate the Latin. He growled at Myrtle and headed off inside.

"You'd think Red would be more appreciative," said Myrtle.

Miles raised an eyebrow.

"We're finding murder victims before poor unsuspecting members of the public do," said Myrtle in a self-righteous voice.

"I rather think of *myself* as a poor, unsuspecting member of the public."

Myrtle said, "You and I are practically pros at this, Miles."

They watched as Red came briefly outside to string up crime scene tape. Then they turned as they heard a vehicle approach.

"Oh, wonderful!" said Myrtle, beaming. "It's Lieutenant Perkins! I've been wondering when I might connect with him."

The state police officer, a tall and wiry man with a military haircut, climbed out of his vehicle and came right over to Myrtle and Miles. "Pleasure to see you both," he said. "Although I'm sorry about the circumstances."

"Me too," said Myrtle. "Isabella was a lovely woman. And a friend of Red's wife."

"I'm sure she'll be very upset at the news," said Perkins.

Myrtle looked somber. "I'm sure Elaine will. I suppose I should break it to her in person after I get back home."

Perkins said, "Could you both give me a quick rundown about what brought you here today? Unless you've already given all the details to Red."

Myrtle rolled her eyes. "Red is being especially irritating today. We only gave him the briefest of background before he went stomping away into the winery. I certainly didn't *plan* on discovering a body today. Miles drove me over here so I could write an article about Serenity Springs and a profile on Isabella for the newspaper."

Perkins nodded. "I see. You were trying to negate the adverse publicity she'd gotten lately."

"That's right. It can't ever be good for business when someone is poisoned at your winery." Myrtle paused, giving Perkins a canny look. "Strychnine, wasn't it?"

Perkins looked a bit surprised. "Did Red fill you in?"

Myrtle snorted. "Red wouldn't fill me in if his life depended on it. It was obvious to me. Gerald was quite contorted, you see. It seemed a most unnatural way to perish." She now tried to affect a vacuous look. "I don't suppose you picked up any forensic evidence worth mentioning?"

Perkins was on his guard by now, though. "Unfortunately, I can't really discuss the evidence we've collected."

"But there is some."

Miles shifted uncomfortably at Myrtle's pushiness.

Perkins didn't seem disturbed by it, however. "We were fortunate enough to find some, yes. Perhaps it'll help us when the case ends up going to trial." He seemed to be trying to get Myrtle back on track for answering questions instead of asking them. "So, you came over to do an interview. Was this arranged in advance, I'm guessing?"

They moved out of the way as an ambulance and several more police cars drove into the parking lot.

"That's right. Isabella said late-morning would be fine. Miles drove me over, as I said. We walked inside to find the winery completely silent. The door chimes when you walk in, so we expected Isabella to come out from the back and greet us."

Perkins said, "You didn't think she might be out in the vineyard?"

Myrtle shook her head. "Not with an interview scheduled. And Isabella seemed keen to get some free publicity. *Good* publicity, that is."

Perkins nodded. "And Mr. Bradford? Could you describe what happened next?"

Miles looked anxious about being put on the spot. "Well, we waited for a minute or two. I was going to sit over by the fireplace and relax for a bit. Myrtle looked around the side of the bar."

Perkins directed his attention back to Myrtle. "What made you do that?"

"I had this premonition, I suppose. Something didn't seem right. So I looked around the side of the bar." Myrtle sighed. "That's when I saw Isabella. She'd been stabbed with a knife. Or maybe it was more like a sickle. It looked like the kind of tool one might use in a vineyard. Wooden handle, curved steel blade."

They heard footsteps behind them and turned. Ben Foster, the manager at Greystone Grapes, was there. The young man cleared his throat nervously. "Sorry. I just—well, I saw the police cars and wanted to make sure everything was okay."

Perkins's attitude now seemed cooler now than it had just moments earlier. He pulled out a small notebook. "Unfortunately, things aren't okay at all. Isabella Montague has been murdered." Perkins was studying Ben's reaction.

"What?" the young man took a step backward. "That's impossible."

"I'm afraid it's not. And I'm glad you came over. I'd like to ask you some questions."

Ben nodded, looking pale. "I don't know anything, though. Like I said, I just came over because I saw all the emergency vehicles coming down the road."

Perkins said, "Sometimes we know more than we think we know. First off, I'd like a little background. Can you tell me where you were last night and this morning?"

Ben flushed. "I was at the vineyard."

"This vineyard?"

"No, no. Greystone Grapes. I was tired out yesterday and turned in early."

Perkins nodded. "Physical labor can do that to you."

Ben looked uncomfortable. "I didn't actually work outside yesterday. I was busier trying to figure out what my next move was going to be, just in case everything started going south."

"Do you know what's going to happen to Greystone Grapes now that Gerald Greystone is gone?"

Ben shook his head. "I spoke to Julia briefly yesterday. She wasn't sure what Gerald's will specified in terms of the vineyard. I think she was supposed to speak to her dad's lawyer today. Of course, she'd love to keep the vineyard going. Julia's just not sure if that's in the cards yet."

Perkins jotted down a note. "Have you spoken recently to Isabella?"

Ben froze for a second. It was clear to Myrtle that he certainly had. Perkins remained silent, waiting for his answer.

"Isabella called me on the phone yesterday."

"Was that unusual?" asked Perkins.

Ben paused. "It wasn't too unusual for her to reach out, no. She liked to call and 'pick my brain,' as she called it. But when she called me yesterday, the topic was a little different from usual."

Perkins just waited.

Ben cleared his throat. "She asked if I wanted to join her team. To work for her at Serenity Springs."

"What time was that conversation?" asked Perkins.

"That was sort of different, too. It was late for a call from Isabella. Nearly nine o'clock at night."

"You may have been the last person to speak with her," said Perkins in his clipped voice. "How did she seem?"

The idea that he might have been the last person to speak with her seemed to shake up Ben even more. He frowned, thinking his answer over. "She definitely seemed frustrated. Isabella had put all this time and effort into making the winery work, then she had this awful publicity. She needed to open the winery back up for business in order to start making money, but she was worried it wouldn't look good."

Perkins tilted his head questioningly. Ben said, "Isabella thought it wouldn't seem respectful to open too soon after Gerald's death."

Perkins nodded. "So she was worried about her business."

"That's right. She seemed anxious, in general. She'd had a long day out in the vineyard yesterday. The temperatures had been warmer than a normal October, and it had been dry. Isabella said she was worried about her vines' health and the cost of watering."

Perkins said, "I'd imagine that would be something you'd be concerned about over at Greystone Grapes, too."

"Of course. But we're well-equipped to handle it over there. Our vines are a lot more mature, hardier. Plus, we have a state-of-the-art irrigation system. Gerald didn't spare any expense, but then it was a well-established business. A new business, like Isabella's, would be sure to struggle more." Ben paused, thinking. "She was also concerned about the labor shortage. She was having a tough time with shift coverage at the winery and getting enough help in the vineyard, too."

Perkins said, "So she asked you to come onboard."

"Right. She just sounded really dispirited. I mean, it's tough to own your own business. She said she needed the help and realized she was treating me like a sounding board way too often. Isabella said it would be a weight off her mind if I joined her team."

Perkins said, "But you didn't?"

"I told her I'd have to think about it. It wasn't that I didn't like or respect Isabella. I think she has had a great selection of wines. She'd done a great job. But I still felt a sense of responsibility toward Gerald's vineyard. I wanted to see how everything was going to play out there. Also, if I left Greystone Grapes, I'd feel like I was leaving them in the lurch." Ben colored a little.

Myrtle suspected he was especially worried about ditching Julia. He wanted to see if she was going to be left in charge of the business and what her plans might be. Ben knew Julia had plenty of bad memories of the business because of her father and the way he hadn't let her be a part of it. But there would also have been a lot of wonderful memories from when she was young. It seemed to Myrtle that Julia was planning on taking the helm of the vineyard instead of putting it up for sale. But Ben wouldn't know that for sure. And he had his future to think of.

Perkins said, "Was anything else on Isabella's mind?"

Ben considered this. "Well, she seemed worried about security."

Miles winced. Considering what had happened to Isabella, it was clearly a valid concern.

Ben continued, "That seemed totally normal to me. After all, somebody had just been murdered on her property, even with all those people around. And then she was by herself at Serenity Springs the past few days, and it was probably on her mind a lot."

Myrtle thought Ben was holding something back, though. What he was saying made sense, but it was the way he was saying it.

Perkins apparently thought the same. He said, "You sound like you think something else was on her mind."

Ben shrugged. "I don't know for sure. But last night, I wondered if Isabella knew something."

"Why did you think that?" asked Perkins.

Ben hesitated. "Because she said something about people lying about where they were. Something like that."

Myrtle and Miles looked at each other. Perkins leaned in a little. "On Saturday? The day of the murder?"

"Yes. She was muttering something about someone lying about not being at the tasting."

Perkins said, "But you didn't get any more information about that?"

"No. It was getting late, and I'd had a long day." Ben flushed again. "Now I feel bad about it, you know? But at the time, Isabella was fine. I told her to lock her doors when she was at the winery and to call me if she got worried about anything. But she'd given me a lot of food for thought, and I wanted to think about it before I turned in."

Perkins's voice changed a little, becoming chattier. "One more thing. I know folks in this town like to talk. There's some gossip going around that you and Gerald were getting upset with each other. Arguing."

Ben sighed. "Maybe we just weren't seeing eye to eye. It wasn't like we were at each other's throats or anything. Basically, I disagreed with Gerald's vision for the business. But surely everybody who's gossiping has got to know that I wouldn't resolve the problem by killing Gerald. What purpose would that serve?"

"Maybe they believe you weren't exactly thinking it through," said Perkins in a thoughtful tone. "Maybe they thought you were reacting in the heat of the moment. Anger can do that to you."

Ben shook his head. "If I disagreed with Gerald that much, I'd have just found another job. There are plenty to be had, even if Serenity Springs hadn't worked out. I'm young, and I don't have any family. If I'd had to move, I'd have just moved. I wouldn't have lashed out at Gerald."

Perkins said, "But you did argue with him."

"Sure. He had big dreams, but didn't seem to have any respect for the land. Gerald only saw it as something for him to squeeze money out of. It just wasn't right."

Myrtle could tell that Ben was getting aggravated just thinking about how Gerald treated the vineyard. He clearly cared a lot about the land.

Perkins said, "Okay. Have you thought any more about who might have done this to Gerald?"

Ben gave a short laugh. "Yeah, I've thought about it. I haven't thought about much else. It's keeping me up at night and distracting me at work. I don't really know anything, of course. But I keep having this gut feeling that Liv was involved in this somehow. If you think Gerald and I were arguing with each other, you should have seen Gerald and Liv. They were much worse."

Myrtle cleared her throat. "When I was speaking with Gerald's daughter Julia, she didn't seem to care much for Liv, either."

Ben eagerly agreed. "You know what I think? I think Liv was totally out of her depth in that relationship. Maybe Liv was rough on Julia because she was jealous of her upbringing. Liv didn't have the same background that Gerald and Julia had. Liv didn't have the expensive education that Gerald had. She hadn't traveled like Julia and Gerald, so she didn't have the expansive worldview. She also didn't read like Gerald did, so she was at a disadvantage there, too. Gerald would host these big dinner parties."

Perkins asked, "You went to those?"

"A few of them. Liv would drink way too much, probably to take the edge off. Then she'd glare at Gerald while he flirted with other women." Ben paused as if he was about to speak a blasphemy. "I don't even think she *liked* wine. She was always drinking fruity cocktails."

Then Ben looked at his watch. "I've got to go get back to the vineyard." He frowned. "Do you think there's really a security risk? Does somebody have some kind of weird vendetta against winery owners? Or their employees?"

Perkins said smoothly, "I think you'll probably be okay. We're looking at all sorts of motives, but these deaths seem personal. We're looking at the circle of acquaintances. But you should always be mindful of general safety, of course."

Ben nodded. "Right." He gave Myrtle and Miles a smile, then headed off.

Perkins watched him go, then turned to Myrtle and Miles again. "So good to see you two again, although I'm very sorry about the circumstances. Be sure to take care of yourselves." Then he too was gone, hurrying off to join Red and the forensic team inside.

Chapter Twelve

Myrtle and Miles climbed into the car. "Well, that didn't go exactly as expected," said Miles with a gusty sigh.

"No, it sure didn't. And now I need to give poor Elaine the news."

"Red won't do that?" asked Miles.

Myrtle made a face. "Oh, he'd do it, but Red is too used to giving people bad news. I think there might be a certain lack of compassion there. Better that she hears it from me."

She jumped as her phone started ringing from the depths of her large purse. "Oh, it's Wanda," she said with a smile.

Wanda was a friend of Myrtle's and a cousin to Miles. She was also a gifted psychic, who often gave Myrtle tidbits that could offer her a new perspective on an investigation.

"Wanda!" Myrtle said as she answered the phone.

"Hi there Myrtle," drawled Wanda. "Figured yew'd probably be done with the winery by now."

It was always sort of startling when Wanda said things like that, although Myrtle knew full and well that she had a gift. "Mercy. You know about the murder at the winery?"

"Know about both of 'em," said Wanda. "Jest didn't know about them before they happened."

"Yes, I know: the Sight doesn't work that way. I have to say that the Sight isn't particularly accommodating."

Wanda chuckled. "Nope. Wish it was." Wanda paused. "What you two doin' this afternoon?"

Myrtle said, "The only thing on my agenda is to write a story for Sloan on Isabella's murder, and that can easily be pushed off until later."

"Think we could go to that used car place?" asked Wanda.

"Well, of course we could! You're ready to pick one out?"

"If Miles can help," said Wanda, sounding a little shy. "Don't know much about cars."

"Neither do I. But Miles would be delighted to help."

Miles gave her a sour look, not entirely sure what Myrtle was committing him to.

Myrtle continued, "We're in the middle of nowhere right now, though, and nowhere near your place." Wanda's home was in the middle of nowhere, too, but in an entirely different section of it. "We'll head back to my house, then over to pick you up. Does that work for you?"

Wanda, sounding quite chipper, confirmed that it did. Miles, on the other hand, was looking rather gloomy at what sounded like quite a bit of driving.

Myrtle hung up and said, "We're going to help Wanda find a used car. Since you are our resident car expert, I volunteered for you to assist us."

Miles looked somewhat relieved. "I suppose it could have been something worse. I wasn't sure what kind of errand it was." He also looked rather pleased at being called an expert.

They got back to Myrtle's house first, because Myrtle told Miles there was something she needed to pick up. She came back out lugging a gnome in a tote bag.

Miles hopped out of the car to take it from her. "You were about to topple to one side, carrying that thing."

"I was not," said Myrtle with dignity.

"What are you doing with this? You're giving a gnome to Wanda?"

"I'm not," said Myrtle, "although that's not a bad idea. I want us to drop this by Greener Pastures. They could use a touch of whimsy on their property. Plus, I feel Red would realize I'm sending a message."

They got back into the car. "Does Red frequent Greener Pastures? It doesn't seem like his usual stomping ground."

"Oh, they call him over there all the time. Residents will tell him that the staff is stealing their things. Stuff like that. Yes, I think it'll prove to be a nice statement."

Miles grew quiet as they started out on the lengthy drive to Wanda's house. "Something on your mind?" asked Myrtle.

"I'm going to do my best to ensure Wanda gets a good car and isn't taken advantage of. But I'm not very sure about my mechanical abilities."

Myrtle snorted. "I think you'll do just fine. You were a mechanical engineer."

Miles blinked at her. "You actually remembered my former occupation."

"Well, of course I did! For heaven's sake."

Miles said, "Although I wasn't a *mechanical* engineer. I was a civil engineer."

"Which means you're good at understanding how things work."

Miles said, "If those things involve bridges, tunnels, roads, and water systems. Cars are a bit outside my purview. I'm thinking I should take the car to a mechanic."

"Should you?" Myrtle frowned. "That sounds expensive."

"Not as expensive as buying a lemon. And I'll pay for the mechanic to check it over. It's important to make sure that there isn't anything wrong with the car. For all we know, it could have been flooded at some point."

Myrtle suspected that Miles's imagination was running away with him. But she knew so little about automobiles that she meekly nodded.

"I'm also concerned about whether Wanda has a valid license. Historically, either Crazy Dan or I have functioned as her driver," said Miles. Crazy Dan was Wanda's brother. He'd recently married and moved out of the hubcap-covered shack the two of them had shared for years.

"True," said Myrtle slowly. "I can't say I've ever seen Wanda drive. Hmm."

Miles said, "Also, are we absolutely certain that Wanda can afford a car? Even a used one?"

"Well, I'm not conversant with her financial situation, aside from the fact that it's definitely improved. She has that wealthy client, you know. Wanda's forever doing video calls with her. It sounds as if Wanda saved up a bit of a nest egg."

Miles looked worried again. "We'll just have to find out what her budget is. I don't want to cause any financial stress. Used cars can be fairly expensive."

Miles continued to fret over the duration of the drive. Myrtle nodded at the right times but didn't feel nearly as concerned as Miles was. Out of all the people she knew, Wanda was one of the few who had her head screwed on straight.

They finally pulled off the old highway into Wanda's dusty driveway.

"I want to see inside Wanda's place now that Dan's out of there," said Myrtle. She climbed out of the car.

Miles sighed, looking as if his entire day had been hijacked.

Myrtle tapped on the door, and Wanda immediately appeared, giving her a gap-toothed smile. Myrtle beamed at her. "I'm so glad you called, Wanda. It's been quite a day, and I feel a distraction is in order."

Wanda nodded soberly, stepping back to let Myrtle and Miles inside. "Seemed like it wuz pretty bad. That poor gurl."

Miles, out of habit, patted his pant pocket to make sure his handy bottle of hand sanitizer was ready and waiting. But when they walked inside the little shack, they both looked around in wonder.

"Wanda!" said Myrtle. "It's completely transformed."

The stacks of horded clutter that Crazy Dan had been responsible for were gone, as they had been when Myrtle and Miles had last visited. But the biggest changes were the homey touches—a crazy quilt carefully placed on the sofa to cover up some of the holes. There were candles everywhere. Old photos had been framed and put on tabletops. Wanda had expanded her collection of houseplants. And perhaps most importantly, everything was clean and shiny.

Wanda gave them a shy smile. "Thank you. Been working hard on it."

Miles looked around him as if unsure where he was. "Did you *paint*?"

Wanda nodded. "Them cigarettes I smoked, they made the paint kinda dingy. So I done painted."

"Well, it looks absolutely amazing," said Myrtle. "I wish you'd taken before-and-after pictures, because it looks like a totally different place."

Wanda flushed, looking pleased. Then, perhaps to get the attention off herself, she said, "Thanks to y'all for takin' me to the car place. Didn't think I'd better go alone."

Miles shifted uncomfortably. "About that, Wanda. I did have a couple of questions for you before we go."

Wanda grinned at him. "Kin I afford it and do I have a license?"

Miles looked startled. "Your psychic abilities at work, I presume."

"Nope. Jest common sense. Figured you might worry about that." She carefully pulled a license out of her pocket, with a photo of Wanda looking stressed but relieved.

Myrtle said, "That's wonderful! I didn't even realize you drove."

"Don't, really. But Dan always made sure I done updated my license."

Myrtle said, "That's surprisingly organized of your brother."

Wanda shrugged her thin shoulders. "More like he wuz worried he'd need me to drive if he had a heart attack."

"Ah. Well, self-motivated or not, it's very helpful," said Myrtle.

Miles said, "And your budget? I'd like to make sure you can comfortably afford the payments on the car. It's not fun stressing over payments."

Wanda bobbed her head in agreement. "Yeah. Reckon I kin pay five hundred a month. Mebbe more, but that might push it."

"Let's not push it," said Miles. "Also, I was telling Myrtle that I'd like to take any car you're interested in to a mechanic, just to check it over. Myrtle has some sort of errand to run, so we can shop at the dealership, drop the vehicle off with my mechanic, then run her errand."

Wanda looked thoughtfully at Myrtle. "The gnome."

Myrtle beamed at her. "Correct! We'll just run over to Greener Pastures where I'll drop off my whimsical gnome to cheer up the poor residents."

Wanda looked even more thoughtful. "That old lady lives there."

"Many old ladies live there," said Miles.

Wanda said, "That one whose son lives by the dead woman."

Myrtle said, "You're really on the ball today, Wanda! Yes, Frank Hayes's mother does live there. Her name is Eunice. I'm sure she'd like to visit with us while we wait on the mechanic to give Wanda's car a thorough examination."

So they set off in Miles's car. Miles frowned. "Myrtle, it suddenly occurred to me that the proprietor of the dealership is in jail."

"Hmm? Oh, right. Yes, Boone Epps is in jail. Or prison, one or the other. But the used car dealership is in new hands now. I'm not sure exactly how the sale happened, considering the Eppses who *aren't* dead are in prison. Except for Rose, of course. But the sale did indeed happen and now Johnny Sims is running the show."

Miles nodded. "That's a good thing. And you won't have any horrible flashbacks, being back there?"

The used car dealership had been the scene of a particularly harrowing event that Myrtle was fortunate to escape from with her life. But she shook her head. "Not a bit. That's the nice thing about people being in jail. They're not around to cause you issues anymore."

The dealership was a fairly large one. Johnny Sims had done his best to make it look cheerful. Multi-colored flags blew merrily in the October breeze. There was a large sign with "Sunny Auto Haven" in large script at the front entrance.

Miles had just pulled into a parking spot when a salesman with bouncy black hair came bouncing out the door. Miles sighed. "Here we go."

"We might as well start the process," said Myrtle. "Wanda, maybe we should walk a lap around the dealership first and you can tell me what you like."

"Ain't that salesman gonna tell me what I want?" said Wanda dryly.

"Miles will waylay him," said Myrtle.

Miles sighed again.

The salesman, Jeremy, was very, very happy to find out Wanda was the buyer. He was even more delighted to find that Wanda wasn't exactly automobile-literate. However, when Miles took over the discussion part, Jeremy was somewhat less excited.

"Let's take that walk," said Myrtle to Wanda.

The two women left the men behind. Wanda looked a little overwhelmed by all the choices. "Yew know anything 'bout cars?" asked Wanda.

"Not much," said Myrtle. "How about if you find five cars you like the look of in your budget, and then Miles can narrow it down to a couple to test drive."

"Test drive?" Wanda appeared taken aback by this.

"I believe that's the customary practice."

Wanda still looked askance. "Drive a car I don't own?"

"Correct. The idea is that you'll enjoy driving some cars more than other cars."

Wanda shook her head. "Don't wanna drive a car I don't own."

Myrtle considered this. "Well, we could have Miles drive it. You could sit in the front seat and the salesman could sit in the back with me. It'll work out just fine."

Wanda didn't seem certain of this, but went ahead and accompanied Myrtle on a tour of the dealership. She quickly identified five cars that she liked the looks of.

"Excellent!" said Myrtle, beaming at her. "I knew you weren't one of those fussy shoppers who can't make up her mind. Let's let Miles and that Jeremy know what you've decided."

Miles listened carefully to Wanda. He recommended three of the cars she'd mentioned. Apparently, the others had some sort of bad press regarding safety issues or some such. The salesman swept them away to one of the Miles-approved vehicles.

"Now, this one is a dream," Jeremy said. "Here, sit in the driver's seat."

Wanda looked alarmed.

"Not to drive, just to sit there," said Myrtle.

Wanda nodded, then took the driver's seat. Jeremy said, "This one has wonderful options that I know you'd enjoy. We have another of these babies that's fully loaded. Remote start, keyless entry. There's a built-in wi-fi hotspot we can enable."

"Don't need it," croaked Wanda.

Jeremy gave her a million-watt smile. "What drew you to this particular car?"

"The color was purty."

Jeremy said, "Indeed it is! I can tell you're a very discerning customer."

Miles cleared his throat. "I don't think the car needs to be fully loaded."

Jeremy asked, "High-end sound system?"

Miles shook his head.

"Built-in GPS navigation?" asked the salesman hopefully.

Myrtle snorted. "She's a psychic. She knows where she's going."

Jeremy carefully overlooked that comment. "All right. So, are we ready to take this car on the road?"

Miles looked at Wanda. Wanda looked at Myrtle. "Myrtle an' I wuz thinkin' you could drive, Miles. I'll set in the front. Mebbe Jeremy an' Myrtle in the back."

Miles frowned. "Don't you think it's better if you drive the car, Wanda? That will give you a much clearer idea about whether you like the ride."

Wanda shook her head, looking bashful.

"All right," said Miles, kindly. "I'll drive."

Wanda, vastly relieved, got into the passenger seat. Jeremy got into the backseat, talking up the car the whole time. Myrtle got in beside him.

When Miles started the sedan, the radio blasted heavy metal at him, scaring the life out of everyone. Miles swatted the radio's power off. Jeremy gave a weak laugh. "Sorry about that. Looks like someone must have left the radio on."

Myrtle muttered, "It would have been a bad sales tactic if you'd given your customers heart attacks."

Miles pulled cautiously out onto the road. Jeremy was directing Wanda to try out some of the features. But the buttons seemed to confuse Wanda. She gamely tried out a few of them, then shrugged, listening to Jeremy and watching Miles make his careful way down the street.

After a minute, Wanda looked alarmed. "Seat's hot. I break somethin'?"

Miles couldn't bring himself to hazard a glance, instead focusing completely on the road. Jeremy leaned up from the backseat. "That's your seat warmer. Great, isn't it?"

Wanda looked as if she wasn't entirely sure she wanted her seat warmed.

"You can turn it off with that button right there," said Jeremy, now practically fully in the front seat as he pointed to it.

Wanda turned it off. The confusing buttons might have meant the end of that particular model because when they returned to the parking lot, she asked to see a different car. Fortunately, that test drive went a good deal smoother. The buttons were less-confusing, the car drove comfortably, and Wanda was smiling.

Back at the dealership, after conferring with Wanda out of earshot of Jeremy (who was gamely trying to sell Myrtle on a vehicle, as well), Miles said they'd like to run the car briefly by his mechanic.

Jeremy looked delighted by this. "Of course! You're a shrewd businessman. Take it and get your man to check it out from top to bottom. Excellent idea."

Myrtle thought Jeremy was entirely too springy. He was starting to remind her of Tigger from Winnie-the-Pooh.

Miles drove the used car to the garage, with Myrtle following in Miles's car. This made for a fairly slow procession. But they finally reached the mechanic, dropped off the car, and were told to return in an hour.

"Onward to Greener Pastures," said Myrtle. She looked back at Wanda. "And I know you get mobbed there whenever we go. You could stay in the car if you wanted. Or take a walk around the grounds. I believe there's a fairly decent walking trail, if the retirement home hasn't allowed it to deteriorate."

Wanda said laconically, "No, I'll go in with you. It'll be okay."

Miles said, "How are things at Greener Pastures these days, Myrtle? I know you have a couple of spies over there to fill you in."

"They apparently made a few high-profile updates." Myrtle rolled her eyes.

"Whut kinda updates?" asked Wanda.

"Stuff that doesn't matter a bit. Greener Pastures tries this kind of thing from time to time. They made some cosmetic changes to their landscaping and building façade. They updated their signage. I hear they purchased some fancy furniture for the commons area. Oh, and they're calling it Greener Pastures Retirement *Village* now." Myrtle gave a short laugh. "As if it's some sort of resort, instead of a place that serves seniors children's food like subpar mac and cheese and beans and franks."

Miles said mildly, "Those seem like nice updates, though."

Myrtle sniffed. "It would be better if they could fix the *real* problems. The horrid food, the rooms that need updating, and lack of staff."

Wanda asked, "Whut changes would you make?"

"Have wine tastings, jazzy music in the halls. Good food, of course. Events that aren't as stale as the stuff they put on now. Make it a place where the seniors are residents instead of inmates."

Myrtle continued on her rant until they pulled into a parking place. She glowered at the new signage. Then she grabbed her tote bag with the gnome.

"I'll take that," said Miles quickly. "If you take a bad tumble, you could quickly end up here permanently."

"I'd like to see Red try," growled Myrtle.

"Where were you thinking of putting this?" asked Miles. Now that he had the tote bag, it occurred to him he was more a part of Myrtle's plan than he really wanted to be.

"A spot of prominence," said Myrtle. "Right over there in the courtyard."

Miles was hoping for a less-conspicuous spot to deposit a plaster gnome. "The spot that every single window overlooks?"

"We're not committing any *crimes*, Miles. We're donating a gift that will cheer the residents up immensely."

Miles was still hanging back. Wanda shrugged her thin shoulders. "I'll do it."

"Really?" asked Miles, looking incredibly relieved.

"Least I kin do, after you helpin' me today." Wanda took the bag from him and strolled over to the middle of the courtyard. She seemed to be carefully calculating the best place. Choosing one, she gently removed the gnome from the bag and placed him in front of a flowerbed. The little guy wore a backpack and carried a map. Wanda patted him on the head and loped back toward Myrtle and Miles.

Miles said, "That's your traveler gnome."

Myrtle nodded. "It symbolizes the spirit of adventure and exploration. Maybe it will inspire the inmates to embrace new experiences, even within the confines of the retirement home. Or to leave Greener Pastures altogether for a cruise. One or the other."

Wanda joined them again, and they walked inside Greener Pastures. Myrtle strode up to the front desk. "We're here to see Eunice Hayes. Could you give me her room number?"

Chapter Thirteen

The attendant smiled at Myrtle. She was clearly new and had not experienced any of the rabble-rousing activities Myrtle had engineered in the past. "Actually, Mrs. Hayes isn't in her room right now. I saw her on my way over here. She's in the puzzle room."

As the three followed the attendant's directions, Myrtle scoffed, "A puzzle room. I wonder if they polled the residents about what they wanted the room to be. Maybe it would be better suited for a video game room. Or a computer lab. Or a library. The thing is, they don't ever seem to take the inmates' wishes into account."

Miles said, "I think a puzzle room sounds rather nice."

Myrtle pursed her lips. "Of course you do."

After wending their way through the maze of hallways, they found the room. Inside, there was an elderly lady with snow-white hair and a pleasant expression on her face. She was not working on the cityscape puzzle on the large table, but rather on her knitting. It appeared to be a scarf.

"Eunice?" asked Myrtle quietly.

The old woman looked up quizzically, but calmly. "Hi there," she said.

"It's Myrtle Clover," said Myrtle gently. "How are you doing?"

"Fair enough," said Eunice. "Although I've been waiting for the flight out of here."

Miles seemed startled, but Myrtle took this in stride. "Have you? And the flights have been canceled?"

Eunice blew out a sigh. "That's right. I've been stuck here in Nicaragua. This vacation has gone on far too long."

"It would be easier if the food was better," said Myrtle.

Eunice made a face. "Those hot dogs and baked beans. Yuck."

Myrtle said, "These are my friends, Miles and Wanda."

Eunice gave them a polite smile before turning her attention back to Myrtle. "You seem very familiar."

"We used to teach together, you and I."

Eunice said, "Did we? Did you teach science, too?"

Myrtle shook her head. "I was in the English department."

"Right, right," said Eunice hurriedly, hastily trying to cover up the fact that she'd forgotten.

Myrtle said, "I saw Frank the other day. He seems like he's getting along pretty well."

Eunice smiled. "He is, isn't he?" She looked down at her lap, appearing surprised by the scarf and the knitting needles she'd laid down there. Then she smiled again, remembering. "This scarf is actually going to be for Frank. He lost his."

"That's what men and boys do, don't they? I remember my Red coming back from school without his jacket more than once."

Eunice nodded, picking up the needles once more. "Yes. Frank will need this for the playground, for sure."

A passel of old women came into the room. One of them said, "That's Wanda! The psychic!"

Eunice happily returned to her knitting, seemingly forgetting the conversation she'd been engaged in.

Myrtle gave the old women a steely look before murmuring to Wanda, "You don't have to do a single parlor trick. I can get rid of these old biddies in a second."

But Wanda shook her head. "It's okay. Might give 'em some entertainment."

The women gazed pleadingly at Myrtle. Myrtle said, "Ten minutes."

They gave an excited squeal and quickly swamped Wanda as Myrtle and Miles took a seat by the puzzle table. Soon, they could hear Wanda saying, "Miz White, you lost a family recipe. It's in yer blue notebook. Got stuck in there."

Mrs. White thanked her profusely and hurried out the door to find it as Wanda moved on to Mrs. Monroe and an ancestor's spirit.

Myrtle watched her carefully. "She seems a bit better now, doesn't she?"

Miles was carefully putting puzzle pieces into the correct spots on the cityscape. "Hmm? Wanda, you mean?"

"Yes. Usually, when Wanda's in a group of harpies like this, she looks unhappy and exhausted. But right now she seems composed and more energetic."

Miles looked up from his puzzle to study Wanda. He nodded. "Bet that's because Crazy Dan left. Now that she doesn't have to deal with the stress of living with her brother, things are looking up for her. Now she has more energy to pour into everything else."

"That's actually a very perceptive comment, Miles."

Miles said, "She might also be relaxed because she has real income coming in. Not only is she being paid by Sloan for the horoscopes, she's also got that wealthy private client. Worrying about money takes a lot of time and energy."

"You've decided she's doing all right, then? Financially?" asked Myrtle.

"I don't think she's swimming in it, but she seems to be a whole lot better off than she used to be. Especially if she can easily swing five hundred dollars a month for a car payment."

Myrtle nodded. "Right. Because she doesn't have to deal with her brother's online buying habit." She was watching Wanda as Miles worked on the puzzle for a few moments. Then Myrtle's gaze was diverted by someone walking through the door. She sat up straighter. "It's Frank Hayes!"

Miles glanced up. He and Myrtle gave Frank a wave. He looked rather confused at the group of elderly women huddled around Wanda. He came over to join them at the puzzle table.

"What's going on?" he asked. "Is Greener Pastures holding an actual event?"

Myrtle scoffed. "As if. No, this is a spontaneous event that my friend Wanda kindly agreed to. Nothing to do with the retirement home."

Frank sighed. "I was hoping to hear that they'd actually planned an activity my mom might enjoy or find stimulating." He paused. "What are you two doing here? Making a reconnaissance mission?"

Myrtle said stiffly, "Certainly not. I have no desire to leave my home. No, we're here because I donated some whimsical yard art for the residents' enjoyment. Then, knowing your mother was here, I decided to have a little visit with her. I didn't realize Eunice was living with dementia."

Frank sighed. "Some days are better than others. How did she seem to you today?"

"She didn't recognize me, but she seemed happy overall. She's knitting away over there and seemed content. Does she like it here at Greener Pastures?"

Miles gave Myrtle a warning look. Myrtle sometimes felt it was her mission in life to convince people to leave Greener Pastures.

But Myrtle blithely proceeded. "It's just that the food is so terrible. And the activities are silly, as you just pointed out."

Frank held out his hands as if making his case. "I didn't want her to come here. I wished she could stay at home. When I felt like she wasn't safe by herself, though, I had to make the choice."

"Well, she does seem happy."

Frank leaned forward as if someone could possibly overhear them in the chaos of women pestering Wanda for answers to the questions of their hearts. "I heard you two found Isabella."

"I'm afraid so."

Frank shook his head. "It's all such a terrible shame. I just can't believe it."

Miles said, "It sounded like you spent time over there regularly. It must have come as a shock."

"It was a really relaxing place to go," said Frank. "Isabella was always welcoming. Not just welcoming, she was funny, smart, and easy to talk to."

"Have the police been by to talk with you again?" asked Myrtle sweetly.

Frank looked startled by the question, and Myrtle continued. "It's their standard procedure, you know. If they spoke with you after the first death, they should do so following the second."

"I suppose you should know," said Frank. "After all, you're the mother of a cop. But the police only spoke to me the first time because they thought I could provide useful information."

"Are you sure that's why they spoke with you?" asked Myrtle, just as sweetly. "I thought perhaps it was because of your contentious relationship with Gerald. At least, that's what people are saying."

Frank's face flushed at this. "People in this town will talk about anything. They're all gossip-mongers." He looked nervously across the room at his mother, still happily knitting away. "I just hope the gossip won't reach Mom's ears. It might kill her."

"We certainly wouldn't want that. Maybe the police would give you a pass if you were able to produce an alibi, Frank. Perhaps you were visiting your dear mother?"

Frank shook his head. "Mom sleeps in until lunchtime. Sometimes the staff has to rouse her to get her to the dining hall before it closes. I was just at home."

"Not on plumbing-related calls?" asked Myrtle.

"There were no calls this morning."

Myrtle said, "Well, that's certainly very unfortunate. Here's another question for you. When was the last time you saw Isabella? Considering, of course, that you frequented Serenity Springs often."

Frank considered this. "I suppose it must have been Monday. I knew Isabella was having a tough time, and that she was worried about her business. Serenity Springs hasn't been open for very long." He looked glum suddenly. "I wonder what will happen to it."

"How was Isabella on Monday?" asked Myrtle.

Frank looked a little irritated. "Like I said, she seemed worried about the business. I was over there just making sure she was okay. I told her how sorry I was that everything had gone poorly. I knew Isabella had a lot riding on the wine tasting."

Myrtle tilted her head to one side. "You mentioned that a little last time."

"What?"

"That you thought Isabella might have had something to do with Gerald's death. Since she had so much invested in the tasting and Gerald was likely going to write a very negative review," said Myrtle.

When Frank spoke, his tone was chilly. "I didn't really think that. I'd just mentioned that Gerald had been unconscionably rude and inconsiderate to Isabella when all she was trying to do was learn the ropes."

Myrtle said, "I've heard the same thing from at least a couple of people. What I don't understand, though, is why Isabella would have started out in the business without knowing how to run it. She didn't seem like the kind of person who'd try that."

"No, of course she wasn't. Isabella told me herself how much research she'd done. Not only that, she'd worked at other vineyards to try to get experience. That doesn't mean that she wasn't going to run into unexpected issues, though. Of course she'd have wanted to ask Gerald to guide her through some of them. He'd been in the business for decades."

"I see," said Myrtle. "So there were just some things that cropped up."

"Yes. But some of those issues were pretty big deals. The vineyard's first vintage had all kinds of problems, according to Isabella. There was some kind of severe pest infestation that affected the muscadines and grapes. Gerald had already gotten a sample of the new vintage and was planning to write some kind of scathing review. I guess he was at the tasting to see what else he could write about."

Miles asked, "Did you talk to Gerald about the reviews?"

Frank snorted. "I avoided Gerald as much as possible. But Ben Foster filled me in when I saw him coming into work one day. Ben was worried Gerald might cause Isabella's business to go under. Gerald had given Ben the review to read. Gerald had complained about the wine's off-putting flavors."

Myrtle frowned. "Everyone seemed to like them."

Frank shrugged. "I liked them, too. But I'm no wine connoisseur."

Miles said, "Nor do we own a competing vineyard."

"Right," said Frank. "Gerald might have had an ulterior motive. Anyway, Gerald was going to publish that the wine tasted like 'rotting fruit' and 'vinegar.' He was also going to mention that the vineyard failed to address quality control issues."

Myrtle pressed her lips together in annoyance at the dead Gerald. "That seems really over-the-top."

"It was," said Frank. "And according to Ben, a review like that could have damaged the vineyard's standing in the wine industry. Serenity Springs could have lost a lot of sales and prestige. I'd known, from things she'd said before Gerald's death, that she'd asked Gerald for tips, and he hadn't helped out. I got the rest later."

"It seems pretty clear Isabella had nothing to do with Gerald's death, considering she's now deceased herself. Any other ideas?" asked Myrtle. She glanced over at Wanda, still in the melee, to make sure she continued to be all right. She was relieved to see that she was focused and in charge of things.

Frank blew out a breath in a thoughtful manner. "Well, I suppose Julia Greystone would be a prime suspect, wouldn't she? Looks like she had lots to gain. I don't really know her, of course. Mama used to tell me Gerald was pretty awful to his daughter. When Julia was a little girl, she'd come over to Mama's house for kind words and cookies."

"That was very nice of her," said Miles.

Frank smiled. "Mama loved mothering strays of all kinds. She took in a baby squirrel that had gotten separated from its mom one time. I guess she thought Julia was much the same."

Myrtle asked, "What did Eunice say about Gerald and his daughter?"

"Just that Gerald acted like he didn't have the time for Julia. She wondered if he'd ever wanted children to begin with. Mama said Julia's mother wasn't much better, either. She was too wrapped up in dealing with her unhappy marriage to give Julia much thought."

"Thank goodness Julia had your mom then," said Miles.

They looked over at Eunice. She'd fallen asleep over her knitting.

Myrtle gave Frank a stern look. "You need to keep up with your scarves. Your mom is working hard on them."

Frank quickly reached into his pocket and pulled out another knitted scarf. "Mama is just confused," he said in a chilly voice. "I don't lose my stuff."

Myrtle decided it was time to vacate Greener Pastures before a staff member tried herding her into a room. "It was good seeing you, Frank. And your dear mother." In a loud voice, she said, "Wanda is now leaving the building. I repeat, Wanda is leaving."

There was a disappointed groan from the crowd, which had grown significantly since Wanda had started. Myrtle took Wanda's thin arm and guided her out of the puzzle room while women continued throwing questions at her.

"We'll charge admission next time," said Myrtle grimly. "What chaos. Are you all right, Wanda?"

"Yep, Was fine. We don't have Miles with us, though."

Myrtle looked behind her. "Did we lose Miles in the maelstrom? Why does he have such a hard time keeping up?" While they waited, Myrtle fiercely guarded Wanda. An old man approached her to ask something, and Myrtle hissed at him.

Miles finally caught up with them. "Sorry," he said, looking flushed. "My shoelace was untied, and I was worried about falling. Then someone asked if I wanted a tour of the facility. I had a hard time getting away from them."

"For heaven's sake," said Myrtle. "Let's get out of here. I feel like Greener Pastures is trying to grip us in its evil clutches."

Miles made haste as he pulled out of the parking place and away from the retirement home. "To the dealership." He looked in the rearview mirror at Wanda. "You're sure you like this car?"

Wanda said, "Yep. It'll do jest fine."

"And the payments are all right? I'll see if I can negotiate it down, of course, but if I don't get anywhere, you'll be able to afford them?"

Wanda said, "Reckon so. I done did the math on it."

"All right. If the mechanic says the vehicle checks out, we'll head back to the dealership and do some haggling."

Fortunately, the mechanic said the car was in tip-top shape. They headed back to Sunny Auto Haven in two cars.

Jeremy was waiting for them. He stepped out, grinning. "What's the word on the car?"

Miles said, "Looks like it checked out. The lady would still like the car."

Jeremy looked over the moon at this statement. "Wonderful! Let's go ring it up."

Miles put the brakes on him. "Let's go to your office and talk about the price."

Jeremy's face fell. "Oh, this is a haggle-free zone. The price on the window is the price of the car."

Miles shook his head. "I don't believe so. I took the liberty of pulling up the market value of the car on the Kelley Blue Book site. Sunny Auto Haven has overpriced the vehicle. Also, I couldn't help but notice the car wasn't in pristine condition."

Jeremy turned to Wanda with pleading eyes. "You said how much you liked the car."

Wanda said dryly, "Miles is talkin' fer me."

Jeremy seemed very sorry to hear this. He turned back around to Miles. "Yes, let's meet in my office to discuss it."

In the end, Miles was able to get Wanda quite a decent discount. The paperwork took forever. Myrtle entertained herself by pulling out a crossword puzzle book from her huge purse. Wanda, scrawling her name over and over again, looked relieved when the process was finally over.

"Congratulations," said Jeremy, giving his million-dollar smile. "You're the owner of a beautiful car."

Wanda looked very pleased. Miles looked pleased too, although he had one question for Wanda when they left the building. "How are you going to get home?"

Wanda looked surprised. "Drive muh car."

"But you didn't want to drive it earlier."

"Wudn't my car."

Miles said, "I see. Excellent. Would you like to practice in the parking lot before you head on the main road?"

Wanda shook her head vigorously. "Nope."

Wanda apparently didn't like the idea of the rows of cars for sale acting as targets for her amateur driving. Miles carefully drove her car out of the parking lot, and Wanda then climbed into the front seat.

"Be careful," said Myrtle. "Are you sure you don't want to do driving practice with Miles?"

"Used up enough of y'all's time today." Then Wanda gave Myrtle a serious look. "Yer in danger."

Myrtle blew out a sigh. "Naturally. Anything else?"

Wanda took the question at face value and seriously considered it. "I see th' danger, but not the person behind it." She squinted hard, as if the person's face was right in front of her. "Nope. Don't got it." She paused. "Be nice to Erma."

"Oh no," groaned Myrtle, as an image of her rat-faced neighbor popped unbidden into her head. "Anything but that. I'd rather just be in danger."

"Jest be nice." And with that, Wanda drove carefully away. Her driving pace made Myrtle look like a speed demon in comparison.

Just minutes later, Miles pulled into Myrtle's driveway. "Looks like Erma is on her way over now," said Miles. "Which is my cue to get out of here."

"Miles!" said Myrtle.

"Wanda didn't tell *me* to be nice to Erma," Miles pointed out reasonably. He left post-haste.

Myrtle squared her shoulders and faced her grinning nemesis. "Whatcha doing, Myrtle?" she asked.

"Oh, just heading into my house." Myrtle's voice was fervent with the hope that she could take refuge in her small house as soon as possible. But Wanda's voice rang in her ears. She took a deep breath and steeled herself to be nice.

"Right. Hey, do you have any tips for dealing with nail fungus?"

Myrtle shook her head. "Not in my wheelhouse. Perhaps a podiatrist?"

"Do you have the number for one? Somebody you recommend?"

Myrtle said through gritted teeth, "Fortunately, I haven't needed one." She glanced over at Erma's yard. Then she frowned. "Erma, it looks like you've been getting rid of some of your shrubs." This, in itself, was not a bad thing. Erma's shrubs were hollowed-out things, a patchy green on the outside and mere sticks on the inside. However, Erma's method of eliminating them seemed odd.

"Tippy said they were dead. Guess I'll be replacing them."

Myrtle said, "It looks like you're using a hoe."

"Well, I've been cutting them back with shears first. Then I use my hoe and yank them up." Erma looked down at her red, mottled hands, which appeared to be bearing the brunt of the activity.

"Would you like to borrow my shovel?"

Erma grinned at her. "Well, sure! I left mine out and it rusted ages ago, and I keep forgetting to get a new one. Thanks, Myrtle. That's very nice of you."

As Myrtle retrieved the shovel, she ardently hoped that this was as nice as she needed to be to Erma and would satisfy Wanda's vision, whatever it had been.

Chapter Fourteen

The next morning, Myrtle studied her pantry. She was feeling as if she should cook something for Julia. The poor young woman had lost her father and was likely working through some very challenging feelings. A special casserole would make life easier to sort out.

Myrtle's pantry, however, was in sad shape. There was no cream-of-chicken (or mushroom or celery) soup. There was no rice to be had. And there was a meager number of canned vegetables. Myrtle supposed she could do something with canned asparagus and a box of instant potatoes, but for the life of her she couldn't figure out what that something might be.

She decided a trip to the store was in order. Ordinarily, when setting out on a big trip to the grocery store, she'd call Miles or Red to drive her. However, Miles might be cranky when asked to tote her around again today, and she certainly had no desire to spend more time with Red. She could only venomously hope Red was enjoying the gnome show she was providing in her front yard.

So Myrtle set out on foot with her cane and a recipe in mind. Pasha joined up with her halfway, loping along beside her as if to keep her company. Or, perhaps, to guard her from danger. There seemed to be plenty of it afoot, after all.

When Myrtle reached the doors to the store, she looked down at Pasha. Pasha gave her an inquisitive, feline smile. "You're right, they should allow comfort cats in the grocery store. They're not particularly enlightened, are they? Maybe you could wait for me and join up on the walk home."

Pasha seemed to consider this seriously. Then she bounded off into a wooded area behind the Piggly-Wiggly after a squirrel.

By the time Myrtle was walking through the aisles, she couldn't precisely remember all the things she wanted to purchase. She remembered the rice and the canned soup. But what vegetables and what protein? Did she have milk? She'd been distracted and hadn't checked her fridge to see what she had. It was all very annoying.

She was standing there, scowling, when someone approached her in front of the meat counter. "Miss Myrtle?"

Myrtle turned to see Liv Anderson, staring at her in concern. "Is everything all right, Miss Myrtle?"

"Oh, it's all just fine, my dear. I was just trying to dredge my memory for the ingredients I needed for a recipe. The dredging is a fairly arduous activity at my age, I'm afraid." Myrtle peered closer at Liv. "I hate to mention it, but you seem rather out of sorts yourself. Are you okay?"

That was apparently all Liv needed to vent. "Julia moved up the deadline for me to get out of the winery. I had to crash on someone's sofa last night. She told me to come back today and get all my stuff. It's unbelievable."

Myrtle's frown deepened. "Heavens. Do you have a place to stay?" She wasn't at all sure she wanted to offer to house a potential killer.

She was relieved when Liv said, "Now I do. I made some phone calls as soon as it was a decent time this morning. I toured a little apartment not far from here. It was *okay*. But I didn't have much time to shop around, did I? If Julia had just allowed me to move out later, I could have compared different apartments. Instead, I'm stuck with that one." She gestured to her cart. "And of course I have to set up a whole new kitchen. So I have to get all the basics to cook. Spices and the whole shebang."

Liv certainly had a cart full. Myrtle couldn't help but notice that there was quite a bit of alcohol in there. It was all beer, too, and no wine. It appeared Ben Foster was right, and that Liv wasn't a fan of wine.

"What's more," continued Liv, intent on extending her rant, "the police are hounding me. Why on earth would I have wanted to kill Isabella? I didn't even know the woman."

Myrtle said sweetly, "Perhaps the police thought Isabella had seen something when Gerald was murdered. The killer would have wanted to eliminate that risk, of course."

Liv threw her hands up in the air. "Well, I had nothing to do with it, regardless of what they think. I was at Greystone trying to collect my stuff, since Gerald's bratty daughter changed the rules on me."

"Did anyone see you there?"

"Nobody else was there," said Liv. "Julia sure wasn't. She didn't want to see me any more than I wanted to see her. Maybe she was out murdering Isabella."

"Still, that's a pity that you don't have a good alibi. That would really have helped convince the police you weren't involved."

Liv sighed. "I told them I hadn't been over to Serenity Springs at all. I'd only met the woman once or twice. One time, Isabella showed up at Greystone to get advice on some vineyard pests or something. I went to find Gerald, and he was no help at all."

"Were you surprised Gerald didn't help Isabella out?"

Liv shrugged. "It was typical Gerald. He wasn't the most helpful of guys. Plus, he thought Isabella was competition. He said something like it took him years to figure out how to run a vineyard and Isabella wanted it handed to her on a plate."

Myrtle said, "So you didn't see Isabella aside from that?"

There was a fleeting look on Liv's face that Myrtle couldn't quite read. Liv shook her head.

"Do you have more thoughts on who might have done this?" asked Myrtle. "Now there are two poor souls gone. I'm sure one reason the police are speaking with you so often is they're under pressure to get the bad guy behind bars. Who might that bad guy be?"

"Julia, of course. She's the one who makes the most logical sense. She had the most to gain from Gerald's death."

Myrtle said, "Did you ever find out the contents of Gerald's will? You were thinking he'd changed it, keeping Julia from inheriting much, if anything."

Liv's face darkened even more. "Julia rubbed that in my face right after she moved the deadline up. It sounds like Gerald made the appointment with his lawyer, but died before he could change it. Doesn't that sound suspicious? If the cops had a lick of sense, they'd realize just how much motive Julia has."

"And you think Julia killed Isabella, too?"

Liv shrugged. "I don't think we have two killers running around. If she killed Gerald, she killed Isabella, too. Maybe Isabella spotted Julia at her wine tasting and realized later that Julia must have murdered her father."

"Julia and Isabella weren't friends?"

Liv glowered at her. "How do I know? Like I said, I didn't know Isabella at all." Liv's eyes narrowed. "Hey, you seem pretty plugged into what's happening around town. Gossip-wise, I mean."

"I suppose."

Liv said, "Can you tell me what people are saying about me around town? I want to know if I should plan for a long-term rental here or whether I need to think about getting a fresh start somewhere else."

"Well, naturally, people talk. They're not just talking about you, though. They're talking about everybody."

Myrtle had the feeling she'd given Liv the kind of bait that would make her ask more. Sure enough, Liv quickly asked, "What are they saying?"

"Just that you and Gerald were squabbling with each other often. That your relationship was somewhat on the rocks."

Liv scowled. "It was probably that boy gossiping, the one who's always mooning over Julia."

"Ben Foster? The vineyard manager?"

"That's the one." Liv brooded. "He thinks I'm mean to Julia. He'd say anything to throw me under the bus."

Myrtle played up the old lady role again. "How very sweet! A little romance in our midst. Does Julia feel the same about Ben?"

Liv snorted. "Julia feels the same about Julia. She's someone who thinks more of herself than anyone else." Liv narrowed her eyes. "Wait, didn't you write an article for the paper on Gerald's death?"

It was quite a late realization on Liv's behalf. But then, Myrtle suspected she wasn't much of a reader. She'd likely only gotten a copy of the newspaper because Gerald's murder was on the front page.

Myrtle looked as innocuous as a nearly six-foot-tall woman could be. "I'm on the staff at the *Bugle*, yes."

"You realize our conversation is completely off-the-record, don't you?"

"Naturally, my dear," said Myrtle, blinking innocently. "You can't imagine a fine newspaper like the *Bradley Bugle* would ever stoop to publishing hearsay, surely."

Liv looked as if she weren't at all sure about that. "Just as long as we're clear on that."

"Perfectly. And now, I think I should finish my shopping trip. Very good seeing you, Liv."

With that, Myrtle toddled off, looking as harmless as she possibly could, feeling Liv's gaze on her back as she left.

The conversation with Liv had somehow managed to wear Myrtle down a bit. Perhaps it had been the vitriol in Liv's voice when she spoke about Julia. Regardless of what it was, it didn't put Myrtle in the mood to cook a casserole. Something happier was needed. Casseroles could be rather dreary-looking. Maybe cookies were in order. She hadn't baked anything since the cookie exchange at Christmas and that had gone exceedingly well.

With this change of direction, Myrtle quickly gathered what she remembered as the necessary ingredients to make cookies. Then she set off back home with Pasha, who had indeed waited for her.

Pasha was apparently in the mood for a little something to eat. She padded in after Myrtle, looking fetchingly up at her as Myrtle put her groceries in the kitchen.

"Snack time?" asked Myrtle.

Pasha's eyes gleamed as she gave Myrtle a feline grin.

Fortunately, Myrtle had remembered to pick up a few cans of cat food at the store, because she was completely out of tuna. Pasha didn't *prefer* cat food over tuna, but she was very polite and ate every single bite.

There was a tap at the door, and Myrtle opened it to reveal Miles, looking particularly well-rested. She was glad she hadn't woken him up that morning to accompany her to the store.

Miles gave Pasha a leery look. He'd had some warm moments with Pasha, but still considered the cat quite unpredictable. "How are things going over here?" he asked.

Myrtle said cheerfully, "They've been excellent. I've already been to the store to buy ingredients for my next masterpiece."

Now Miles seemed even more troubled. "What sort of masterpiece?" he asked with some foreboding.

"Cookies for Julia. I've been quite remiss in not bringing her any food. The poor thing lost her father, after all. I know the two of them weren't close, but his death is probably giving Julia all sorts of conflicting feelings. Cookies are sure to help."

Miles winced, which Myrtle didn't notice because she was looking into the mixing bowl where she was dumping butter and sugar. Miles said, "Doesn't Julia have a lot of leftovers? That funeral reception had gobs of food. I'm guessing she went home with it."

"That doesn't mean she can't have something sweet. I'll admit that I was originally looking to make Julia a casserole. But then I decided cookies might be nice. Something sweet might make life seem a little brighter."

Miles looked very doubtful about this.

Myrtle continued, "Besides, it's fall. Baking is important in the fall."

"Aren't cookies sort of complex to make?"

"What a question, Miles! Of course they're not. They're easy-peasy."

Pasha glided into the room. Her beautiful eyes narrowed as she saw Myrtle adding eggs and liquids to the dry ingredients in the bowl. She pulled her ears back.

Miles frowned at the bowl. "I haven't baked cookies in a while, but I'm not absolutely certain you're doing this right."

"Have you *ever* baked cookies? That seems rather out of your wheelhouse."

Miles said, "I was a very hands-on dad. I did participate in Christmas cookie baking. However, I believe I remember creaming the butter and sugar together." He gave her a nervous look. "Do you have a recipe?"

"In my head." Myrtle tapped her noggin.

"I'd feel a lot better about this endeavor if there was a recipe in plain view."

Myrtle sighed. "For heaven's sake." She puttered over to the cabinet and pulled out an ancient cookbook. Thumbing through it, she found a spattered recipe and pointed it out to Miles.

Miles studied it while Myrtle continued stirring the concoction in the bowl. "This says to use brown sugar."

"Well, I didn't have any of that, so white sugar it is."

Miles frowned into the mixing bowl. "Myrtle, that's powdered sugar."

"Which is white."

Miles knew by this time when arguing was pointless. He bit his tongue and ignored his rising tide of panic. When the cookies were done, Myrtle stacked them immediately on a plate, despite the fact that they should have cooled first. Miles decided he'd just disavow any part of the cookie caper when they arrived at Julia's.

"I assume you'd like a ride to Greystone Grapes," said Miles when Myrtle had carefully wrapped the still-steaming plate of cookies with plastic wrap.

"Yes, please. Of course, I do want to speak with Julia again. I'd like to hear more about her thoughts on Isabella and find out where she was when poor Isabella perished."

"Of course," said Miles, repressing a sigh. "Although we can't guarantee that Julia will be there. It's likely a workday for her."

He grabbed his keys, and they walked out of the door and toward Miles's car.

"She might have taken bereavement leave," said Myrtle.

"You mentioned before that Julia was a pet groomer. It might not be the type of career that offers much leave."

"True. Although she might already have handed in her notice for that. After all, she's apparently in line to receive the vineyard," said Myrtle, climbing into the car.

"Is that a sure thing? I thought there was some doubt about that."

Myrtle said, "There was. But then I saw Liv at the grocery store this morning. She said Julia claimed the will stated she was inheriting Greystone Grapes."

Miles frowned. "I suppose Gerald must not have followed through on his threat to write Julia out of his will."

"I believe Liv said that Gerald had an appointment with an attorney, but he died prior to it."

Miles raised his eyebrows. "That seems convenient. And it makes Julia's motive even stronger."

"I believe so. Of course, there are others with fairly decent motives, too."

Miles said, "I might be in need of a suspect recap. It's hard for me to keep track."

"Well, we have Liv to start out with. We've heard that Liv and Gerald's relationship was quite volatile. Liv denies any issues, but Ben Foster said Gerald was always in a terrible mood following an encounter with Liv. She was said to fling allegations of infidelity at him."

Miles said, "The idea is that Liv got mad at Gerald and got rid of him?"

"That's right."

Miles frowned. "With poison? I can see Liv lashing out in anger at Gerald, but it's hard to picture her putting strychnine in his wineglass."

"Gerald could be very vituperative. Besides, Liv seemed to think she might benefit from Gerald's will. She said something at the reception about Gerald wanting to provide for her."

"That sounds like wishful thinking to me," said Miles.

"Perhaps. Then we have Ben Foster, the manager and winemaker of Gerald's vineyard. He felt very strongly that Gerald was taking the vineyard in the wrong direction. They'd been arguing about the issue. Ben felt Gerald was too focused on developing the vineyard into a large, commercial production. Ben was more interested in quality and small batches."

"Again, though, can we picture Ben poisoning his employer? That seems a rather harsh reaction to the problem," said Miles.

"But there's more to it than that. Ben is also completely smitten with Julia. Gerald has been treating Julia horrendously. Perhaps Ben decided to take things into his own hands."

"I suppose," said Miles. "Poisoning still seems particularly harsh. And isn't it a woman's weapon?"

"Or an excellent weapon for anyone who wants to walk away from the crime scene before the victim dies. Let's see, where was I? Oh, yes. Frank Hayes."

Miles said, "He seemed rather innocuous the times I've met him. Although I don't think he was fond of Gerald."

"He certainly wasn't. Frank blamed Gerald for pushing his mother into selling family-owned land that she'd cherished. He thought that her regret over that sale made his mother spiral, resulting in her move to Greener Pastures."

Miles considered this. "It seems like quite a stretch."

"Yes, but you're thinking clearly. Frank clearly isn't. His emotions are making him see things differently. He was also angry with Gerald for hosting such loud gatherings on his property. Bands, crowds of people, and whatnot."

Miles said, "That would annoy me, too. You think you have a nice, quiet place to live and then there's basically a circus next door." He paused, thinking. "I suppose the last suspect is Julia Greystone."

"Right. And she has an excellent motive. Julia was eager to live at the vineyard. She basically said it had always been her happy place. That she'd never pictured herself anywhere else. Then her father banished her from Greystone Grapes. What's more, he acted as if she was too incompetent to run the family business."

Miles shook his head. "I can't imagine where he came up with that. I've only briefly met her at the service, but my impression was very good."

"Well, we're about to spend more time with her in a few minutes." Myrtle paused. "Going back to why Gerald thought Julia couldn't run the vineyard. Maybe Gerald was angry Julia was closer to her mother than she was to him. Julia told me when her parents divorced, she'd definitely have stayed with her mom if it hadn't been for the vineyard."

Miles said, "Was Gerald the type of person to hold grudges? Or to be very petty? Because that's pretty petty."

"I think he was the sort of person to hold grudges, yes. And it sounds as if he had the capacity for pettiness. But Julia wasn't just upset with her dad for not allowing her to live at the vineyard. She might also have been alarmed at Gerald's threats to change his will."

Miles said, "That would have been such a vindictive thing for Gerald to do."

"Yes, but it's in line with his character. And Julia wanted that vineyard. It certainly constitutes a motive."

They pulled into the long driveway leading to Greystone Grapes. The wind was gusting, making the trees around them sway.

"We're not supposed to have a storm, are we?" asked Miles, frowning. He wasn't much of a fan of storms, particularly when he needed to drive in them.

"In October? That would be out of character for Bradley. I'm sure we'll be just fine." Myrtle stepped out of the car, carefully balancing the plate of cookies. She didn't seem to notice that the cookies, not having been allowed to cool, had clumped together. And, with the shifting of the car, some of them had fallen apart.

They walked into the Greystone Grapes tasting room. It was completely different from the Serenity Springs one. When Myrtle and Miles stepped inside, they were greeted with clean lines, minimalist décor, and a cool toned color palette. There was abstract art on the walls. Myrtle gave a small shiver. It seemed very cold and clinical. She wondered if Julia had plans to change it up.

A staff member walked out to greet them, and Myrtle asked to speak with Julia. Soon, Julia joined them, smiling as she strode up. Despite the smile, Myrtle noticed Julia seemed exhausted. There were lines around her mouth and her eyes looked bloodshot.

Chapter Fifteen

"We brought you some cookies, dear," said Myrtle. "Just to let you know we've been thinking of you."

Miles quickly added a disclaimer. "The cookies are courtesy of Myrtle. I didn't bake them."

Julia gave Miles a curious look, but continued smiling. "Well, that's very kind of you, Miss Myrtle. I appreciate that. These will make for a nice break for me."

"Oh, have you been working? We're not interrupting anything important, are we?" Myrtle managed to look both sweetly concerned and rather vulnerable, as if being hurried out the door would hurt her feelings terribly.

Julia quickly said, "Let's have a seat, why don't we? I should probably take a break, anyway." She led them over to some very modern chairs. Myrtle wasn't at all sure they were certified as comfortable for octogenarians, but was surprised when she sat down. They were a good deal comfier than they'd originally appeared. Whether she'd be able to extricate herself *out* of the chair was another matter altogether, however.

Julia gave Myrtle and Miles a bright smile. "I've just been working at going through my dad's stuff."

Myrtle tsked. "Such a difficult task."

"Not really," said Julia blithely. "It's been strangely cathartic. Also, I feel as if I'm doing something good for mankind because there is a huge amount of clothing that I can donate. They're nice clothes, too." She rolled her eyes. "I've also been throwing out the stuff Liv left behind."

Myrtle said, "Oh, Liv isn't living here any longer. Did she forget to pack many items?"

"Old makeup, mismatched socks. And some of the 'artwork' Liv created when she was intoxicated," said Julia in a disparaging tone.

"Is Liv an artist?" asked Miles.

Julia snorted. "*She* thinks she is. And now I have to lug it to the dump."

"May I see some of the art?" asked Myrtle.

Julia stood up. "Absolutely. Beauty is in the eye of the beholder, after all. Maybe you'll like something, and I'll be spared having to toss it out." She strode from the room to collect it.

Miles said, "Myrtle, why on earth would you want bad art? I thought you had enough of that when Elaine was working through her art hobby."

"Well, I'm not opposed to getting free décor, as long as it's not completely frightful. But I'd also like to sneak into Liv's mind a little. Maybe we can get a clue as to what was going through her head by viewing her art."

Miles appeared doubtful at this. And indeed, Julia returned with a couple of canvasses with paint slopped on them with no apparent rhyme or reason.

Julia laughed at Myrtle's expression. "I told you they were bad."

"Are they like that on *purpose*? Or did Liv suffer a mild stroke in the middle of creating them?"

"Who knows?" said Julia, giving the canvasses a disgusted look. "Even the impressionistic one is a mess. I guess she got worse when she drank too much. Don't worry, I'll load them in the car with the rest of the stuff that's heading to the dump." She dropped the paintings unceremoniously on the floor, then sat in another of the chairs. "I suppose you heard about Isabella."

Myrtle said, "Yes. Miles and I were actually the ones who discovered her. Such a terrible tragedy. Isabella was a lovely young woman with so much promise."

Julia's eyes opened wide. "Wow, I had no idea you were the ones to find her. That must have been awful."

"It was quite a horrible surprise. Miles had driven me over to Serenity Springs so I could interview Isabella for the paper."

Julia nodded slowly. "It makes sense that she'd have been looking for positive press. Having a murder at your winery couldn't be good for business." She pursed her lips. "Now there have been two murders there. I'm not sure how Serenity Springs is going to find a way through this."

Miles cleared his throat. "Would you ever consider purchasing the land and winery? As a second tasting room?"

"That would nearly double the size of our property. We'd have to really think about that kind of move." Julia gave them a wry look. "Especially since right now I seem to be a suspect in Isabella's murder. Buying her property would enhance that motive. And it doesn't need enhancing. Although it might be nice if some of the winery's equipment and tools go up for auction. We could use some updated things."

"Are the police giving you a hard time?" asked Myrtle, looking sweetly concerned.

"Of course they are. It's their job to hassle people. But I had nothing to do with Isabella's death."

Myrtle asked, "Oh, were you able to give the police an alibi? That's wonderful."

"I wish I could have. But I didn't have one. I had to get away from the winery because Liv was moving out, and I didn't want to be around her. I was at my own place, packing to move into the winery."

Myrtle said, "How do you feel about all that's happened? I know you loved this place growing up, and there's a lot of family history here. But it's also a spot that's probably created a lot of stress for you in the last few years."

Julia nodded. "I have mixed feelings about Greystone Grapes. There are dark times and happy times all mixed together. I guess I mostly feel ambivalent . . . like I'm waiting to see how I should feel. How it all shakes out." She sighed. "I thought I was going to feel totally different about all of this, you know? I've been waiting to return to the vineyard for years. I thought I'd have a smile pasted on my face the whole time. But instead, I feel this enormous weight on my shoulders."

Myrtle said, "You've taken on quite a mantle, haven't you? All the responsibility for the staff at Greystone Grapes, of course. But you've also got to carry on family tradition."

"Right. And not screw anything up on my watch." Julia paused for a moment, looking thoughtful. "It's been keeping me up at night, too. I've been feeling pretty inadequate. I can't help but wonder if my father was right after all. Maybe I'm just not suited for the job."

"Nonsense," said Myrtle briskly. "There's no one better suited. You love the place and you'll do a wonderful job running it. Besides, you'll have an excellent right-hand man to help you out. Ben Foster is a very capable young man."

Now Miles was frowning at Myrtle. He clearly suspected matchmaking might be afoot again.

Myrtle continued, "I'd imagine it would be easy working with Ben, too, since you both have common interests. When I spoke with him the other day, I was so very impressed with him."

Julia tilted her head curiously. "Really? What did he say?"

"Gracious, some of it might have been over my head," said Myrtle, falling easily into the befuddled old lady again. "But I know he talked about sustainability goals and whatnot."

She was rewarded by a flicker of interest in Julia's eyes.

Myrtle said, "Ben had been concerned about the direction the vineyard had been going in under your father's management. He seems to really care about the quality of the wines."

Julia took this in for a few moments. "Well, that's good to hear. I haven't had a chance to speak with Ben yet since my father died. I mean, aside from very brief phone calls and a couple of minutes at the funeral reception. He asked me to grab a coffee with him after the memorial service, but I was too exhausted to take him up on it. Then I've been so focused on clearing things out of here that I haven't made the time to have a meeting with Ben. I'll go ahead and schedule that."

Myrtle nodded. "After family deaths, it seems as if the list of tasks goes on and on. And you mentioned you've had a rough time sleeping, too."

Julia made a face. "I dread trying to sleep. I think about everything I need to do."

Myrtle perked up. "I have excellent advice for insomnia."

Miles made an inelegant snort as if he were suppressing laughter. Myrtle gave him a cold look. "What is it, Miles?"

"It's just that you have chronic insomnia."

Myrtle said, "And who better to give advice than someone who experiences it?" She turned back to Julia. "You should make a brain dump before you turn in. Grab a notebook and list everything that comes into your head that you need to accomplish. Writing it all down should help clear your mind enough so you can drift off."

Julia said, "Actually, that's great advice. I don't know why I didn't think of it."

Myrtle said, "And make sure you turn your alarm system on at night. I'm sure Gerald had one installed, correct?"

Julia nodded. "It's not something I ordinarily use."

"Under the circumstances, it might be prudent if you turn it on, just for the peace of mind. After all, there have been two murders next door. Perhaps your subconscious is trying to keep you alert to any signs of danger by not allowing you to sleep."

Julia said slowly, "That's a good point. I'll admit, the whole thing has made me a little jumpy. I'm usually a matter-of-fact person, but I've been feeling like I need to watch my back. I'm often at the winery alone while I'm sorting through things."

"Maybe you should bring Ben back to the office," said Myrtle.

Miles rubbed his forehead as if it hurt.

"Again, not a bad idea. I'd thought it would be easier for me to clear things out without Ben being underfoot, but it makes sense to have someone else around."

Miles said, "Of course, you do have a receptionist or bartender at the front."

"Only sometimes, though," said Julia. "We've had limited hours this week." She rubbed her forehead, closing her eyes briefly. "This is all just crazy. I can't believe Isabella is gone. What a nightmare." She sighed. "I feel sort of guilty, too, because I've always felt kind of jealous of her."

"Jealous?" asked Myrtle.

Julia nodded. "Just because she owned a winery and was in complete control of it. Isabella came up with ideas and implemented them. When I looked at my own life, I felt like it fell short in comparison. There were days when I didn't even feel like an independent adult."

"But you had a job, your own money, and a place of your own to live," said Miles, pushing his glasses up the bridge of his nose.

Julia said in a rueful voice, "A low-paying job, very little money, and a place that I rented. But I appreciate the kind words. I loved my job, but it wasn't what I'd dreamed of doing. And there were some months where I had to ask my mom for a little money to help fill in the gaps. I've never felt very successful. But now that I've got the winery, I really want to make a go of it. I want to make sure the vineyard continues thriving, even if it means a lot more sleepless nights. I'd feel awful if the business took a nosedive right when I ended up at the helm."

Myrtle said, "I'm sure you're going to do a marvelous job running the winery. It's what you were born to do, after all." She paused. "Going back to these awful crimes. Have you thought any more about who might be responsible?"

Julia shrugged. "Well, last time we talked about it, I thought it might be Frank or Isabella. It's clearly not Isabella. So now I'm wondering if my instincts are off altogether. Maybe Liv is responsible. She sure was spitting mad when I asked her to clear out. I mean, *really* mad. I was starting to think I could be a crime victim, myself. It's obvious she has a real temper."

"I can imagine," said Myrtle. Then she frowned. "I hesitate to say this, dear, but I've heard some talk around town lately. That your father and you had recently argued, and that Gerald was planning to change his will?"

Julia looked weary. "Probably the same talk the police heard. They've asked me about that, too. I figured I'd already lost the vineyard as soon as he and I argued. Dad was the kind of person who followed through on his threats. I was shocked when the lawyer said he'd left it to me. If there had been any other way to keep the vineyard in the family, I'm sure he'd have written me out of his will. But I was his only child. Dad was an only child too, so he didn't have any siblings or nieces and nephews to leave it to." Her eyes narrowed. "I have the feeling I know where this particular rumor started. It sounds like Liv has been running her mouth. She's a very vindictive person."

Myrtle supposed that being forced to leave one's home at a moment's notice might put someone in a bad mood. But she gave an understanding nod. Then she looked at her watch. "Gracious, we should be letting you get back to your work. Miles and I didn't intend to stay this long. I hope you enjoy your cookies."

Miles gave Julia a weak and apologetic smile regarding the future consumption of the cookies.

"I certainly will. Oh, wait a minute." Julia walked over to the bar and reached behind it, coming back over with two bottles of wine. "One for each of you. I'm so sorry you've had such a rough time lately."

Myrtle looked slightly confused, and Julia clarified. "Finding bodies, I mean."

"Oh, right," said Myrtle. "Yes. Very, very disturbing." Although, of course, it really wasn't as disturbing as it should have been. It had become somewhat habitual.

A few minutes later, Miles and Myrtle were back in the car, heading back. "Did you get what you were looking for from all that?" he asked.

"I think so. It was interesting how Julia was talking about Isabella, wasn't it?"

"Was it?" asked Miles with a frown.

"She just seemed sort of coldly clinical about Isabella's death. Julia appeared more interested in whether there would be an auction for the Serenity Springs' tools."

Miles said, "Well, after all, she'd pegged Isabella for a killer previously. The two women weren't best friends or anything. It sounded like Julia barely knew her."

"She did mention being jealous of her, as well. That Isabella owned a vineyard and had complete control over it."

Miles said, "Considering that was what she dreamed about, I can imagine she was envious." He paused. "I'm taking you back to your place, I'm assuming?"

"We could go out to lunch at the diner. That might be fun."

Miles made a face. "I'm not sure I'm in the mood to have fun."

"Don't be an old fogey, Miles. It's not becoming. What are you in the mood for, if not to enjoy yourself?"

"I thought I'd take a stab at the book club book. The meeting is tomorrow, after all."

Now it was Myrtle's turn to make a face. "Don't remind me. I'm not reading the tripe they assigned for this month."

"Was it that bad?"

"Who knows?" said Myrtle. "I took one look at the cover and decided to pass. It had unicorns on it. Sparkly ones."

Miles quirked an eyebrow. "You judged a book by its cover? That's considered a no-no for readers."

"This particular book was crying out to be judged. Anyway, I was distracted by the theme for this month's meeting."

Miles smiled. "Guilty pleasures?"

"Yes. Who on earth came up with that?"

"Blanche, I believe," said Miles.

"That doesn't surprise me. Blanche is becoming increasingly erratic as she ages. My understanding is that we'll all offer our guilty pleasure reads, then the group will vote on the title they most want to read next month. Correct?"

"That's my understanding," said Miles.

"Why do I have the horrible feeling that our picks won't be chosen?"

Miles said, "I prefer to stay optimistic about our chances."

Myrtle sniffed. "Sadly, I'm older and wiser than you, Miles. No one will vote on our choices. What's yours?"

Miles was cagey. "You'll have to find out at the meeting."

"Then that will be the only interesting thing about book club." Myrtle sighed. "Well, if you're going to be trying to cram in this month's selection, I suppose I'll just piddle around the house this afternoon. Maybe I'll watch *Tomorrow's Promise*." She gave Miles a sideways glance.

"You won't be able to tempt me with the show today. I'm determined to give this month's book a chance."

Myrtle said, "That's very noble of you. And quite surprising."

"It's only because someone pointed out that I hadn't contributed much to the discussion for the last three or four months."

Myrtle said, "Because you hadn't read the books."

"Correct. Last month, Sherry gave me a hurt look when she realized I hadn't read her selection. It occurred to me that perhaps I was hurting people's feelings. That I was being too judgy with what I read."

Myrtle gave him a wry look. "You'll be sorry for being such a gentleman. You're about to suffer an untold ordeal, I promise you."

"You can't tell it's *that* bad from the cover."

Myrtle said, "Just let me know your thoughts when you finish the thing." As Miles pulled into Myrtle's driveway, she groaned. "Erma is working in her front yard again. Maybe she won't see me."

"I thought you were supposed to be nice to her. Per Wanda."

Myrtle said, "But I *was*. I lent her a shovel. That's as nice as I can possibly force myself to be."

Fortunately, Myrtle was somehow able to slink past Erma, who seemed to be whistling off-key to herself as she vigorously worked in her yard. Thanking her lucky stars, she locked the door behind her.

Chapter Sixteen

The next morning, Myrtle readied herself for book club. She felt as though she might need to gird herself in iron for the upcoming foolishness. What was more, Blanche was hosting it. Blanche was fond of having alcoholic beverages out for book club. Since it was morning, Myrtle hoped she'd limited herself to bloody Marys and mimosas. However, she had the feeling that Blanche might expand the selection to a whole host of drinks. It meant that every member was sure to be there, including the dreadful Erma.

Miles had offered to drive Myrtle, but Myrtle fancied a walk. She also didn't want to have to depend on Miles for a ride. It was entirely possible that Myrtle might want to escape early, particularly if the members started getting tipsy. She could only imagine the silliness that would ensue. Miles also had the uncanny ability to get waylaid at these gatherings. The women all thought he was wonderful. Smart, single, nice-looking, monied (at least by Bradley's standards), and he could still drive a car. Those attributes chronically placed him in the most-desirable male category for his age group. The women pursued him relentlessly.

When Myrtle walked into Blanche's house, she could tell that Blanche was indeed in a festive mood. In fact, it looked more like a Cinco de Mayo celebration than it did a book club meeting. There were balloons, streamers, paper lanterns, string lights, and the bar that Myrtle had expected to see. Also, as expected, there was already excellent attendance at the gathering. Several of the women, cocktails in hand, were laughing uproariously at something Blanche had just said. Myrtle stood there primly, her guilty pleasure read in her large handbag.

"Myrtle!" called out Blanche. She wove her way over to her. "The life of the party!"

"The life of the party!" chorused three tipsy women behind her.

Myrtle pressed her lips together.

"Would you like a peach bellini?" asked Blanche. "It's my specialty cocktail today."

Myrtle had the feeling it would behoove her to be quite firm with Blanche from the very start. If one displayed any sign of weakness or wavering, one would end up full of prosecco and schnapps. "No, I have a bit of a headache. It certainly won't improve with alcohol."

Blanche rolled her eyes. "How can you be the life of the party if you don't have a cocktail? Besides, from everything I've heard, you really need one. Is it true you and Miles discovered another body?"

Blanche was really being quite annoying, decided Myrtle. She was always a bit brazen and had the tendency to love life just a little too much, but she was being quite tacky at this point.

"Sadly, yes. Miles and I found poor Isabella Montague. Had you been to Serenity Springs? It's a lovely place."

Blanche gave the smallest of hiccups. "I sure did, right after they opened. I thought it was great. I felt like I was walking into a retreat. The wine wasn't bad, either. But, you know, the place wasn't as *lively* as Greystone Grapes. Gerald really knew how to throw a party."

Blanche had finally whetted her interest. Myrtle said, "I've heard he hosted bands there. Was there dancing?"

Blanche snorted. "Was there dancing? Of course there was! It was like a real party, even when I was around strangers. He had his wines there, lots of great appetizers, stuff like that. Nothing too fancy. Just good bar food." Then she winked slyly at Myrtle. "And some nice eye candy."

"Eye candy?" Myrtle frowned. The mental image wasn't appealing.

"I mean an attractive young man. Ben Foster, the guy who basically runs the vineyard for Gerald. Or he *did* run it, anyway."

Myrtle's frown deepened. Surely Julia hadn't fired Ben. She wouldn't have wanted to see her business go down the drain. And she'd given no indication that she'd let him go when she and Miles had spoken with her. "He hasn't lost his job, has he?"

Blanche shrugged, an energetic gesture that knocked her slightly off-balance. "No idea. But what if he *has*? He's got to have a job. He worked far too hard in school. If he's out of work, he can't pay back his student loans."

"You seem to know an awful lot about Ben's situation."

Blanche said, "Well, I talked to him a lot at the winery. I was curious, you know, what it takes to manage a vineyard and be a winemaker. And he's just so young."

Myrtle suspected alcohol had fueled Blanche's interest.

"Anyway, did you know he worked for a pest control company to put himself through school at UNCC? And he was taking serious subjects like chemistry. How on earth do you study for a degree in chemistry and have a real job at the same time?"

This made Myrtle pay more attention to the tipsy Blanche. If Ben was a pest control expert, he'd surely have been quite familiar with strychnine and its properties. After all, strychnine was a rat poison. Could Ben really have gotten so upset with Gerald that he decided to take him out? She thought of the genial young man, so smitten with Julia, and found it difficult to believe. Still, love can work in mysterious ways. Maybe Ben was tired of Gerald's treatment of Julia and removed Gerald from the equation.

"Anyway," said Blanche. "He might have himself a girlfriend now. I saw Ben and Julia Greystone together at the diner this morning before book club."

Myrtle smiled to herself. She always liked it when her matchmaking was a success. Hopefully, the two young people were discussing something other than winery business.

Blanche was now sauntering drunkenly off to greet other guests. It was a good thing because Miles had arrived and slipped quietly next to her. "Quite the bacchanalian meeting," he murmured.

"Isn't it? Of course, we should have expected as much. Blanche is hosting, and she is rather fond of a party." Myrtle squinted to see what Miles's guilty pleasure read was, but he maneuvered the book behind him so she couldn't see. She sighed.

Miles said, "The meeting will be starting soon, and you'll find out then."

"*Will* it be starting soon, though? I have the feeling Blanche will not prove an effective timekeeper today. Perhaps I'll step in."

Miles nodded. "That might be a good idea. I'm guessing she's not entirely on top of her game right now. I saw the two of you talking when I was coming in."

"She's had a few of her specialty drinks, I believe. But she did actually offer some interesting information about Ben Foster."

Miles raised his eyebrow. "That's surprising. How does she know him?"

"Oh, from cozying up to the bar at Greystone Grapes. He was apparently in there one day while she was enjoying some wine. Blanche mentioned that Ben Foster worked at a pest control company while he was at UNCC."

Miles didn't seem to make the connection immediately. "Okay. So he was a hard worker. That jives with what we've heard about him, doesn't it? He's a skilled manager and winemaker who's in demand. Isabella wanted him to work for her, after all."

"Yes. But the tidbit that was interesting was that he was working in the *pest control* industry. A technician in that field would certainly be familiar with strychnine and its properties. And Ben was studying chemistry, according to Blanche."

Miles considered this. "I suppose a knowledge of chemistry would be important in agriculture. I see what you're saying. Are you going to tell Red?"

"Certainly not! I had to suffer through a conversation with an inebriated Blanche to get that nugget of information. I'm not going to just hand it over to Red. He should work for it."

Miles knit his brows. "It sounds like the kind of finding that you should share with the authorities. Maybe Perkins? You always enjoy speaking with him."

"Dear Perkins! I'll consider it, of course. Maybe he and I can trade off bits of intel."

Myrtle was interrupted from future musings by the sound of cheering as a group of women noisily toasted . . . something. Myrtle pressed her lips together tightly. "This meeting is off-the-chain. I'm going to call it to order before things go even further downhill."

Myrtle walked to the front of the room and summoned her sternest teacher's voice. "Everyone! It's time to start the book club meeting. You can continue with the festivities following our discussion."

Myrtle was sure she heard some mild grumbling, but narrowed her eyes as she scanned the room. Everyone suddenly became very quiet and polite. There was one stray giggle, but a stern look from Myrtle nipped it in the bud.

Blanche hurried to stand next to Myrtle. She beamed at the gathering. "So thrilled to see everybody today," she slurred. "Let's get started by talking about the book we've been reading since the last meeting. Myrtle, since you're up here, what did you make of *Whispers of the Enchanted Unicorn*?"

Myrtle said grimly, "I thought I'd read something else, so I made a different selection."

Blanche laughed uproariously at this. "What did you read?"

"*One Hundred Years of Solitude* by Gabriel García Márquez."

Now the rest of the book club joined Blanche in laughing at Myrtle's pick. Myrtle gritted her teeth, but smiled sweetly in response. "It's a story of human isolation," continued Myrtle. "Which is starting to sound more and more appealing. What I'd like to know is what Miles thought of *Whispers of the Enchanted Unicorn*."

Miles flushed. He looked as if he would much rather discuss Márquez's book. He appeared to be searching his mind for something to say about the unicorn story. "I liked the font on the front cover," he offered slowly.

Myrtle raised her eyebrows. "Any other tidbits you'd like to share with the group?"

Miles cleared his throat and pulled at his collar. "The author's consistent use of the word *enchanted* was . . . enchanting. It certainly drove home the theme of the story." He looked desperately around him. "I'd like to hear someone else's interpretation of the book."

He seemed relieved when Erma Sherman rose her hand to speak.

Erma said excitedly, "I thought it was fun that the unicorns were life coaches. And I liked Sparklehoof, the main character, a lot."

There was a murmur of agreement in the room. Myrtle quickly found a spot in which to sit down. Surely this was a new low for her book club. She suffered through the rest of the discussion, which included such hyperbolic statements as saying the book was a spiritual awakening and that it changed one deluded member's life.

Finally, the discussion came to a merciful close. But then it was time for the next portion of the meeting. The theme for next month.

Blanche, who had somehow gotten even tipsier during the book discussion, thankfully ceded the floor to Tippy. Tippy was decidedly *not* intoxicated and was pursing her lips in disapproval at the general carnival atmosphere in the room. This resulted in everyone settling down just a bit.

Tippy gave them all a tight smile. "Now comes the fun portion of the meeting."

Blanche, perhaps speaking louder than she meant to, said, "It would be more fun if Tippy would have a cocktail." There was some accompanying snickering, which Tippy graciously ignored.

"We're going to announce what our favorite guilty pleasure reads are," said Tippy. "We all have them—the comfort reads that we come back to again and again when life is challenging. Then, as a group, we're going to vote on the best guilty pleasure read." Tippy reached down into a tote bag. "I've taken some money out of our treasury to provide us with some prizes. The winning book will be next month's book club read. We will also offer prizes to the other categories we announced last month, although those titles won't be included on our book rotation."

On a nearby table, Tippy pulled out a bookstore gift card, a pair of socks covered with prints of card catalog entries, and a couple of bookmarks. Myrtle suspected the treasury could have withstood much more expensive prizes. Tippy was always very careful to preserve the balance. Perhaps she was planning on them to go on a book-related field trip. Although Myrtle shuddered to think what type of field trip this group would decide on.

Tippy said, "Now what we'll do is go around the room and name our guilty pleasure reads. I'll go first. I'll admit to a fondness of *The Devil Wears Prada* by Lauren Weisberger. Myrtle, how about you?"

"*Pride and Prejudice* by Jane Austen," answered Myrtle promptly. She waved the book in the air.

Erma commented, "That's a *guilty pleasure* read? That's classical." Erma's voice, perhaps amplified by alcohol, was even louder and more obnoxious than usual.

Tippy seemed to be in quite a snappy mood. "We'll have no denigration of anyone's guilty pleasure reads! Myrtle, I think that's a great pick. Miles, how about you?"

Miles was already looking chastened by the fact classical fiction had been so quickly put down. He cleared his throat. "*Frankenstein*."

Blanche said, "Hey, we were only supposed to pick books! Movies aren't allowed."

Miles and Myrtle exchanged a glance. Miles said, "*Frankenstein* is a book by Mary Shelley. It was written in 1818."

"Well, I never," said Blanche, sounding subdued. "I thought it started in the 1950s with all those monster movies. I learn something new every day."

Tippy redirected them to continue going around the room. There were some Nicholas Sparks books, a Dan Brown, and quite a few romances to round things out. Then everyone voted.

Tippy swiftly counted the votes. She smiled. "The winner is Miles Bradford! He's the recipient of a bookstore gift card."

Everyone applauded. Myrtle sourly suspected that Miles had won because everyone felt sorry for him that Blanche had given him a hard time. Plus the fact, of course, that many of the women in the room were secretly in love with him.

Miles, blushing a little, sat back down next to Myrtle. "Things are about to go downhill from here," she muttered.

Sure enough, the next categories for prizes were "best book swoon", "best cliffhanger," and "most dramatic plot twist," all of which Myrtle and Miles sat out. The books they were accustomed to reading didn't belong in any of the categories.

Miles whispered to Myrtle. "Perhaps we should broaden our horizons a little."

"Are you crazy? I don't want to read the same things they're reading."

"Doesn't that make us book snobs?" asked Miles. He said the words distastefully.

"I'm rather proud of that designation," said Myrtle with a sniff. "I can't help it. I was an English teacher, after all."

"Let's see if we can participate in the next category."

Fortunately, that was "top tearjerker." Myrtle picked *Where the Red Fern Grows*. Miles picked *The Art of Racing in the Rain*.

"We do read modern books," said Myrtle.

"From time to time."

The prize for that category went to Tippy, who picked *The Lovely Bones*.

That wrapped up the meeting. Some women went back to Blanche's cocktail bar, while others hurried to congratulate

Miles on his win and bat their eyelashes at him. Myrtle slipped out the front door and headed back home. She was about halfway there when she heard Erma's voice calling out behind her.

Myrtle winced. She was decidedly not in the mood to speak with Erma right then. Besides, she'd already been nice to her by lending her the shovel. Myrtle knew Erma would think Myrtle's hearing was impaired. It was generally an assumption that greatly annoyed Myrtle, who considered her hearing quite perfect. This time, though, she was happy to have Erma believe in the fallacy. She slipped inside her house and locked the door behind her.

She was horrified to hear a tap on her front door just a minute later. Surely Erma wasn't insisting on a visit? Myrtle peered cautiously out the window. She was surprised to see Frank Hayes there.

She opened the door. "Frank? Is everything okay? How's your mom?"

Frank said, "Oh, about the same. Mind if I come in for a minute? There's something I wanted to tell you that I thought maybe you could report on for the newspaper."

Myrtle definitely didn't want Frank in her home. He seemed to be behaving in a rather shifty manner. "I've had a long morning, Frank. Book club was quite vexing today. Maybe we can speak tomorrow over coffee."

Frank took that opportunity to shove past her and inside her house.

Chapter Seventeen

"What on earth are you doing?" asked Myrtle heatedly. "The very idea! Your mother didn't teach you any manners?" She backed away from him toward the kitchen.

"I'm sorry, Miss Myrtle. It's really not my fault. You've been asking too many questions. And making those cunning remarks."

Myrtle stopped at this. She didn't deny that she was cunning, but she didn't recall being so around Frank lately. Then she stopped short. "Your missing scarf. Your mother was knitting you another scarf when we visited her at Greener Pastures."

Frank stared at her tensely. "You told me to be careful about losing my scarves."

Myrtle continued, her mouth feeling dry. "I suppose you lost yours at the firepit near Gerald. Poor Isabella saw it, recognized it, and realized what it meant. You felt you had to get rid of her."

Tears popped into Frank's eyes. "The whole thing is a disaster. I never wanted to hurt anybody."

"Well, you did a terrible job of not hurting anybody. We're up to a body count of two, and I'm guessing you're planning on me to be number three. Besides, Gerald's death was hardly unintentional, was it? You came prepared with strychnine poison. Which I'm not entirely sure how you managed."

Frank shrugged. "You can get anything online."

"Not rat poison. That's regulated."

Frank said, "Luckily for me, you can buy it as a bait application to control gophers."

"We don't have gophers here."

"That wasn't why I needed it," said Frank calmly. The tears had dried up, and he now took a menacing step toward Myrtle.

"Helloooo!" came a cheerfully nosy voice from behind them. "Door's open! I'm coming in."

Myrtle had never been so glad to hear Erma's voice in her life. Frank swung around to see Erma gaping at them, holding Myrtle's shovel. Myrtle yelled out, "Erma, be careful! Frank's the killer!" then dashed to her kitchen.

Frank looked as if he didn't know whom to attack first. Erma shrieked and started waving the shovel around in a presumably defensive manner. Frank took it in an *offensive* manner, however, and rushed at her.

Myrtle grabbed the wine bottle that Julia had so kindly given her yesterday. With it, she rushed into the living room and found she could disable Frank quite effectively.

Erma's jaw dropped as she stared at the tableau in front of her, still clutching the shovel. "Is he dead, Myrtle?"

"Of course not," said Myrtle in a huffy voice. "He's simply unconscious."

"What do we do when he wakes up?" asked Erma fearfully.

"We hit him again with the wine bottle. Or the shovel. Or both things." Myrtle opened her purse, rifling through it for her cell phone. She punched in a phone number and said pertly, "Red? I need you to come over to the house. I've got your killer for you."

Myrtle hung up. "That'll get him here on the double."

Erma was still frozen. "I was just bringing you back your shovel."

"You were not," said Myrtle crisply. "You were being nosy. You wanted to see why I had a male visitor and who it was."

Erma swallowed hard. "Maybe so."

"I'm glad. Just this time, mind you! I'm glad you came over. You distracted him, Erma."

Erma looked pleased with herself. "I did. I made him look at me so you could get the wine bottle and hit him with it. We make a good team, Myrtle."

"I wouldn't say *that*. I'd say it was quite serendipitous that you came by." Myrtle punched at her phone again. "But now, I think Miles should come over. As my sidekick, he'll want to witness the denouement."

Erma's face twisted in concern. "Should Miles come over, though? Isn't this a crime scene? Aren't we supposed to protect it?"

"It's not a crime scene. No one died."

Erma was peering over at Frank Hayes again. "Are we absolutely, positively sure about that?"

Myrtle pressed her lips together before saying, "If you want to check for a pulse, be my guest."

Erma lay the shovel down carefully and tentatively crept up to Frank, who was indeed lying very still on the floor. She reached out for Frank's neck and he muttered something. Erma screamed bloody murder, leaping backward as if she'd seen a ghost. The scream got through Frank's unconsciousness and his eyelids fluttered open. He groaned.

Myrtle brandished the wine bottle at him. "Stay where you are," she said sharply. "Red is on his way over." With one hand, she completed the call to Miles. "Miles? I've got the killer. Can you come over? There's a lot going on here."

As she hung up, she heard a police car screech into her driveway. "Excellent," she said. "Good timing."

Red burst through the front door as if there was a pack of wild dogs on his heels. "Mama?"

"Right here." Myrtle waved the wine bottle at him.

Red gave Erma a confused look as he hurried over to his mother. Perkins was right behind him. He gave a polite nod to Erma, who tittered a giggly hello to him. Frank was lying on the floor looking very sore and put out.

"Do we need to call an ambulance?" asked Red tersely.

"No," said Myrtle. "Not for that little tap I gave him."

"I was asking Frank," growled Red.

Frank considered this, sitting up gingerly and giving Myrtle a wary look. "No, I'm all right. But she knocked me unconscious with that thing."

"Which was well-deserved," Myrtle said caustically. "He tried to kill me."

"I saw it!" said Erma with delight. "I saw the whole thing. I can tell you all about it. I'm your witness."

Then Miles hurried through the front door, looking perplexed at seeing Erma, the shovel lying abandoned on the floor, the cops, Myrtle with the wine bottle, and Frank, who was looking increasingly sulky.

"It's a zoo in here," Red muttered to Perkins.

Perkins said, "I'd like to hear what happened."

Red quickly added, "I'd like to hear it from the horse's mouth. Frank? What happened? Did you come over here to attack my mother?"

Frank glared at Myrtle. "She attacked *me*."

Erma jumped in. "That man, whoever he is, was going to kill Myrtle. I saw it with my own eyes!"

"Why did you come over with a shovel?" asked Red. He rubbed his forehead as if it was very sore.

"Your mama was very kind to me and lent it for my yard project."

Red narrowed his eyes. "Really? That seems . . . out of character."

Myrtle said in a prim voice, "I can be very kind." Then, as Red continued staring at her, she snapped pointedly, "Wanda recommended I do it." It always annoyed her when Red discounted her friend's abilities. He should know that Wanda helped keep her safe.

Red closed his eyes upon hearing the psychic's name. Miles carefully sat down across the room, far away from the purported killer on the floor, but close enough to see and hear what was going on.

Perkins said, "Frank, it would help us out a lot if you could tell us what happened. What made you come over here today?

But first, let me run down your rights for you." He quickly informed Frank of his rights, which Frank didn't seem remotely interested in.

Frank was now looking tired and defeated. Or, perhaps, Myrtle had given him a concussion. He shifted position again. "Okay. I saw your mom over at Greener Pastures."

Red lifted his eyebrow, looking over at his mother.

"I had a delivery to make there," she said. "A very fetching gnome to cheer up the poor inmates."

Red rolled his eyes, then looked back at Frank. "Continue."

Frank glared at Myrtle. "She was there. Talking to my mother."

"Being friendly to Eunice," said Myrtle with a sniff.

Frank said, "She told me I needed to be more careful where I left my scarves."

"I'm guessing you left one at Gerald's crime scene," said Perkins. "We retrieved one there and kept it as evidence."

"That's right," said Frank, exhaustion dripping through the words. "What she said sounded like a warning to me. I figured maybe she wanted to blackmail me. I knew she didn't have much money."

Myrtle scowled at him. "I live quite comfortably within my means. Not everyone is a criminal like you."

Frank threw up his hands. "Whatever. I'm just saying it sounded like a threat."

Perkins looked thoughtfully at Myrtle. "Why did you mention the scarf? How did you know about it?"

"Eunice Hayes was knitting it for her son because he'd lost it. That's it. That's the story. I was simply reprimanding him for being careless with his belongings. It was his own guilty conscience that turned it into something else entirely. But once I realized Frank was the murderer, everything fell into place."

"Like what?" asked Red.

"Well, like the fact that Isabella seemed rather distracted the last time I spoke to her."

Red said, "That could be explained by the fact that she had just had a murder at her establishment."

"It *could*, but it seemed to go further than that. She mentioned something about having to see after the lost and found items. I thought at the time that she was thinking about all the people at the winery who had to leave in a rush when Gerald's body was found. That they had, understandably, left some of their belongings behind. But now, it seems clear that she'd put two and two together. Frank's scarf had been there, even though Frank had stated he wasn't at the wine tasting. Isabella must have seen it before the police arrived. She'd stepped out to see Gerald's body and came in looking worried. I thought she was simply worried about Gerald's death, but now I'm guessing she was thinking about Frank's scarf."

Red frowned. "Was the scarf that distinctive?"

"Well, you don't see hand-knit scarves very often, you know. Most of them today are flimsy things. It would have stood out, I'm sure. And once Isabella made the connection, she was living on borrowed time. Frank had to get rid of her."

Miles cleared his throat from across the room. "Why didn't Isabella just tell the police?"

Myrtle said, "I'm guessing that she considered it circumstantial evidence. She knew it was Frank's scarf and she knew he'd left it the morning of the wine tasting because she'd have made sure everything was immaculate before the event. But she didn't know if maybe he just slipped next door for a little while and then left. Maybe, in Isabella's mind, Frank might not have had anything to do with the murder. She'd have wanted to give him the opportunity to explain before throwing him under the bus. After all, he was a loyal customer." She looked down at Frank with contempt. "Does that all sound correct, Frank?"

Frank glowered at her. "Yeah. Isabella wasn't flinging accusations or anything. She wanted to find out if there was a reasonable explanation for the scarf being there."

"Which there wasn't," said Myrtle airily. "And you were blindsided. You grabbed the nearest weapon at hand, which would have been the pruning knife Isabella had been using in the vineyard. You availed yourself of it, silencing her for good."

Red said, "Then you ran into Mama at the retirement home, and she seemed in on everything."

"Which I *would* have been if I'd just had two moments to think. It's been very, very busy," said Myrtle defensively.

Frank said, "Yeah. She came home—walking up to the house. I'd parked farther down the street."

Erma jumped in. "She was walking back from book club at Blanche's house." She seemed highly excited at the story she was going to tell everyone once she left Myrtle's house.

Frank shrugged. "Whatever. I knocked on the door right when she arrived."

Perkins said, "That seems bold, murdering someone in the middle of the day."

Erma said, "He's desperate! A desperate, conniving man."

Frank ignored her. "Well, I needed to shut her up. The more I thought about it, the more I was sure she wanted to let me realize she knew something and then make me pay her to keep quiet."

"But you weren't going to pay," said Perkins.

"It doesn't make any sense to pay blackmail. I could have been paying her the rest of my life."

Red snorted. "That was poor reasoning. She's an octogenarian."

Myrtle gave him an icy look.

Erma couldn't restrain herself from hopping in again. "I saw him slink over to Myrtle's house. I could tell he was no good right away."

Myrtle said, "You could tell no such thing. You were simply prying. You saw a man come inside my house, and you were dying to find out who he was and whether I had a suitor. Then you decided to return the shovel I lent you in the hopes of getting information."

"And then I saved your life!"

Myrtle gave her a quelling look. "It was more like you diverted Frank's attention so that I could save myself."

Erma was hugging herself. "I helped," she said in wonder.

Miles was smiling across the room. Myrtle sighed.

Red frowned at Frank. "How'd you get your hands on the poison?"

"Online. You can buy it as gopher bait."

Red said, "We don't have gophers here."

Frank gave him a tight smile. "That's what your mom said. Look, just get me out of here, okay? My head's really hurting.

You can find the poison in my order history. And you guys probably have my scarf, right? I'm sure it's covered with my DNA."

Myrtle said, "Out of curiosity, how did you slip the poison into Gerald's drink?"

"It was a piece of cake. We were just talking for a while outside. There wasn't anybody else out there at the time. He was bragging about all the things he was going to do to develop the land he stole from my mom. Then he got up to use the restroom. When he was gone, I sneaked it into his glass. Then I left. Nobody saw me."

Perkins said, "Well, I think I've heard enough. Let's head to the station and get you booked." He gave Myrtle a warm smile. "You take it easy, okay? That was harrowing."

"Harrowing for *me*," muttered Frank as Red put him in handcuffs.

Myrtle ignored Frank, beaming at Perkins. "I'll certainly do my best. It's been a busy day between an appalling book club meeting and then nearly being murdered."

Red rolled his eyes. "Yes, that makes for a pretty bad day."

Red and Perkins left with Frank between them. When they opened the door to leave, there were neighbors standing on both sides of the street, staring and pointing at Myrtle's house.

Erma rushed to the window to look out and wave at everyone. "Hey, we're famous. They're all going to want to hear the story."

"I'm going to be *writing* about this story as soon as I catch my breath," said Myrtle severely. "But you're welcome to tell a few people about it. Just remember that Sloan likes to sell newspapers, so don't tell *everybody.*" But she knew Erma would. And that the news would spread like wildfire through the small town.

Erma said, "Hey, how about if we celebrate with a drink? We caught a killer, Myrtle! That doesn't happen every day."

Myrtle pursed her lips. "Hasn't there been enough alcohol flowing for one day? Book club was bad enough."

"I only had a small glass of wine there," said Erma. She looked over at Miles. "We deserve a little something, don't we?"

Miles nodded. "I think the occasion calls for it."

"The occasion being?" asked Myrtle.

"Being alive. And sending a murderer off to jail," said Miles.

Myrtle considered this. "I'll open the sherry."

Erma waved her hand at the bottle of wine that Myrtle still clutched in her hand. "How about that wine?"

"This? It's from Greystone Grapes."

Miles said, "I can't think of a better time to open it. I'm sure Gerald would enjoy having one of his bottles here at the moment his killer receives justice."

And so they opened it. And, in a rare moment of solidarity, the three of them raised a glass. "To dodging danger," said Myrtle.

"Cheers!" said Erma.

After excited chattering for a few moments, Myrtle was pleased to find Erma was eager to leave and greet her adoring public, since the neighbors were still clotted on the sidewalks.

Myrtle gave a sigh of relief as she left. Miles stored the shovel away in Myrtle's shed, then came back inside. They sat on the sofa for a few quiet moments.

"*Tomorrow's Promise*?" asked Myrtle.

Miles nodded. "It might be just the thing to watch right now."

And so the two friends spent the next hour watching the familiar but outlandish storylines, relaxing, and sipping their wine.

About the Author

Bestselling cozy mystery author Elizabeth Spann Craig is a library-loving, avid mystery reader. A pet-owning Southerner, her four series are full of cats, corgis, and cheese grits. The mother of two, she lives with her husband, a fun-loving corgi, and a couple of cute cats.

Sign up for Elizabeth's free newsletter to stay updated on releases:

https://bit.ly/2xZUXqO

This and That

I love hearing from my readers. You can find me on Facebook as Elizabeth Spann Craig Author, on Twitter as elizabethscraig, on my website at elizabethspanncraig.com, and by email at elizabethspanncraig@gmail.com.

Thanks so much for reading my book...I appreciate it. If you enjoyed the story, would you please leave a short review on the site where you purchased it? Just a few words would be great. Not only do I feel encouraged reading them, but they also help other readers discover my books. Thank you!

Did you know my books are available in print and ebook formats? Most of the Myrtle Clover series is available in audio and some of the Southern Quilting mysteries are. Find the audiobooks here: https://elizabethspanncraig.com/audio/

Please follow me on BookBub for my reading recommendations and release notifications.

I'd also like to thank some folks who helped me put this book together. Thanks to my cover designer, Karri Klawiter, for her awesome covers. Thanks to my editor, Judy Beatty for her help. Thanks to beta readers Amanda Arrieta, Rebecca Wahr, Cassie Kelley, and Dan Harris for all of their helpful suggestions and careful reading. Thanks to my ARC readers for helping to spread the word. Thanks, as always, to my family and readers.

Other Works by Elizabeth

Myrtle Clover Series in Order (be sure to look for the Myrtle series in audio, ebook, and print):

Pretty is as Pretty Dies
Progressive Dinner Deadly
A Dyeing Shame
A Body in the Backyard
Death at a Drop-In
A Body at Book Club
Death Pays a Visit
A Body at Bunco
Murder on Opening Night
Cruising for Murder
Cooking is Murder
A Body in the Trunk
Cleaning is Murder
Edit to Death
Hushed Up
A Body in the Attic
Murder on the Ballot
Death of a Suitor

A Dash of Murder
Death at a Diner
A Myrtle Clover Christmas
Murder at a Yard Sale (2023)

THE VILLAGE LIBRARY Mysteries in Order

Checked Out
Overdue
Borrowed Time
Hush-Hush
Where There's a Will
Frictional Characters
Spine Tingling
A Novel Idea
End of Story

The Sunset Ridge Mysteries in Order

The Type-A Guide to Solving Murder
The Type-A Guide to Dinner Parties (2025)

Southern Quilting Mysteries in Order:

Quilt or Innocence
Knot What it Seams
Quilt Trip
Shear Trouble
Tying the Knot
Patch of Trouble
Fall to Pieces
Rest in Pieces

On Pins and Needles
Fit to be Tied
Embroidering the Truth
Knot a Clue
Quilt-Ridden
Needled to Death
A Notion to Murder
Crosspatch
Behind the Seams
Quilt Complex

MEMPHIS BARBEQUE MYSTERIES in Order (Written as Riley Adams):

Delicious and Suspicious
Finger Lickin' Dead
Hickory Smoked Homicide
Rubbed Out

And a standalone "cozy zombie" novel: Race to Refuge, written as Liz Craig

Made in United States
North Haven, CT
17 May 2024

52599503R00122